Satanic Static

Bryan Holm

ANUCI PRESS

First paperback edition 2025

Anuci Press edition 2025

www.anuci-press.com

Cover Design by Don Noble

roosterrepublicpress@gmail.com

ISBN 979-8-9914345-9-1 (paperback)

ISBN 979-8-9919612-0-2 (eBook)

Satanic Static

(LE, Gatefold, 2LP, VG+)

An album by Bryan Holm

"The paradox I am.

The equinox extending my hand into dimensions to unlock new doorways.

And so the light has revealed to me that there must be more ways.

And so I play with rhythms."

-Pharoahe Monch.

"I'm still listening to wax,

I'm not using the CD."

-Mike D.

Side A: Intro:
The First Movement
(Notturno Allegro)
(3:51)

1.

Rose was a revelation, and she was forcing Killian to question the path he had been on his entire life. He watched her studying her anatomy textbook as they sat on their usual bench, a blanket over their laps. It was a brisk October day in 1975, the beginning of Killian's second year at Saint John's Catholic University. A sharp breeze blew burnt-orange leaves through the lush green courtyard.

Rose looked up from her textbook, "Can I help you?" she asked, snickering.

"Sorry. Was I staring again?" Killian replied.

"Maybe."

"You sure you can't sneak me into your cafeteria for dinner?"

"Not unless you can fit into one of my skirts." Rose was a freshman in the nursing program, and the uniform was a requirement, even as a student.

"I might look pretty good in one."

Rose sized him up, "You have the figure for it."

Killian pulled his hand out from under the blanket. He held Rose's palm in his own. Rose let go quickly, making sure no one saw.

"Careful! You're going to get yourself kicked out!" Rose said.

"Would that be such a bad thing?"

"Are you serious?"

Killian leaned in quickly and gave Rose a peck on the cheek. She gasped.

"Alright mister, now you're going to get us both kicked out of here!" Rose packed up her things, still beaming, filling her backpack with her books.

Killian checked his watch, sighing, "Hopefully I can drag him out of his cave and get him to dinner at least."

"It's really that bad?"

"I don't think he's showered in a week."

"Have you talked to your professors?"

"It's just *first year jitters*, according to them."

"New York is a world away from Iowa. What do you think?"

Killian put his own books away in a leather satchel. "Ever since he took the job in the archives, he's been different. Doesn't eat, doesn't sleep. I can hear him all night, lying in bed, muttering to himself."

"What's he saying?"

"Gibberish. Something about being afraid of the dark, about running out of time."

Rose couldn't help but laugh. "Well, good luck with that!"

"I know, right?" They stood up.

"Library at eight?" Rose asked.

"Library at eight."

Rose gave him a quick kiss on the lips. Killian stepped back, in mock shock.

"See! *You're* the bad influence in this relationship!"

Rose sauntered away, grinning, "That'll be five Hail-Mary's for you, *Father* Connolly."

2.

Killian was a Bostonian born into a strict Irish Catholic family, and it had been decided early on in life, preordained from birth really, that he would become a priest. Catholicism was a facet of every aspect of Killian's family life growing up, and he had wholly embraced it.

Until he met Rose. Ever since that chance encounter in the library his first week back in seminary, the idea of a solitary life of servitude paled in comparison to a potential life with her.

As Killian got closer to his dorm, a familiar dread overwhelmed him. He hated that it had come to this, that he loathed to be in his own dorm room. He made a pact with himself that it was time to have a heart-to-heart with his roommate Steven, to air it all out. Killian detested conflict like that, but he couldn't take it any longer.

The dread lifted when he got to his door. He could see through the peephole that the room was dark. He went inside, switching on the light. Steven was sitting on the floor, cross-legged, facing the corner.

Killian stepped back, his heart pounding. "Jesus! What are you doing in the dark?"

Steven didn't reply. Killian opened a window.

"No offense, but it smells like a locker room in here. When's the last time you showered?"

Steven stayed silent.

"I'm glad you're here. We need to talk."

Steven rocked back and forth slowly; his greasy hair matted to his forehead.

"Do you hear them?" Steven asked, a whisper.

"Hear who?"

"DO YOU HEAR THEM?" Steven screamed.

Shocked by the outburst, Killian knelt down, placing a hand on Steven's shoulder. "Hey, Steven, you okay?"

Steven wheeled around, brandishing a knife. He slashed at Killian, opening a long gash on his left cheek.

"What the hell!" Killian fell back on the floor, crawling away on his elbows. Steven lunged on top of him.

"You must hear them! You have to! They're everywhere!"

Steven raised the knife in the air, aiming for Killian's chest. Killian shot his hand up, gripping Steven's scrawny wrist. Killian propelled himself up, easily spinning Steven onto his back. As Killian straddled his chest, he realized just how gaunt Steven had become in the last few weeks. The Iowa farm boy had disappeared. It felt like he was sitting on a bag of bones.

"What the hell is wrong with you!" Killian yelled at him.

Killian twisted his wrist, and Steven whimpered, dropping the knife onto the worn green carpet. Steven locked eyes with Killian, and it seemed for an instant that the faint flicker of flames burned behind Steven's bulging eyes.

Killian yelled at their closed door, "Help! Anyone out there?"

Steven shot a knee upwards, connecting dead center between Killian's legs. Killian let out a shriek and flopped onto the floor, cradling himself. Steven jumped to his feet, grabbed the knife, and sprinted out the door.

3.

Killian and Professor Bennett, a clerical collar poking out from beneath his trench coat, patrolled the campus commons in the dark. Bennett was approaching eighty, a brusque man with a King James view of the world and his religion. He and Killian often clashed in the classroom, derailing that day's lesson plan with spirited debates on the role of the Catholic church in modern times.

The quarreling was done with a sense of mutual respect. Bennett saw Killian's inherent intelligence on the first day of class, and Bennett had quickly become a mentor to him. He even welcomed Killian into his apartment on Sunday nights for a home cooked meal and additional lively conversation, something he had only done with a handful of students over the years.

Bennett carried a flashlight, scanning the shadows between the mammoth granite buildings. "You should have come to me sooner."

"I did," Killian replied.

"I didn't know he was this troubled."

"I didn't either, to be honest, not this bad at least." Killian held a damp washcloth against his bleeding cheek.

"You're going to need stitches."

Killian nodded. "After we find him."

"So, he's been in the archives, alone?"

"Every night, way past curfew. Even on his days off, I think."

"Do you know what he does in there?"

"Not really. Something with the audio archives, inventorying reel-to-reels, and vinyl records?"

Bennett glanced at Killian, his eyebrows raised.

Killian stopped, "Look." He pointed towards a small chapel. The only building on that side of the campus that wasn't dark. Candlelight flickered through the stained-glass windows lining the sanctuary. Killian and Bennett hurried towards it.

4.

They entered the chapel slowly. The sanctuary was lined with granite walls, the stations of the cross etched into a macabre border surrounding them. The wooden pews had been shoved aside, piled up against the perimeter. Dozens of candles burned on the stone floor, forming a massive pentagram. Steven stood inside it, behind a long altar.

The altar held three antique turntables and two 8-track players, hooked up to a pair of large speakers. The records spinning on the turntables were thick, 78 RPM acetate records. The center of each was a plain crimson label, all hand-numbered in black ink, #1, #2, and #3.

A deafening static filled the room, bouncing off the walls. Underneath the static, a chorus of dead languages, spoken by children, indecipherable, but seemingly in unison. The 8-tracks played the same thing, recordings of the records, only delayed. The sounds all mixed and swirled together, overlapping in differing pitches, as if the voices were conversing with themselves, creating a terrifying, otherworldly symphony. Killian's blood ran cold. Bennett fumbled for his crucifix.

Steven glared at them, an exaggerated grimace spreading across his face. "You must hear them now?" Steven brought his wrist to his mouth. He tore into his flesh with his teeth, a wild animal tearing at the nerves extending towards his palm.

Killian's stomach heaved. "Steven, what are you doing?"

Steven held out his arm, still smiling, blood and chunks of skin covering his exposed teeth, dripping down his chin. He held his hand over the turntables, slowly moving it back and forth. Blood poured from his jagged wound, soaking the records. They began to spin faster and faster, the sounds in the sanctuary growing louder, the screams more frantic. The blood was being absorbed into the records, disappearing beneath the grooves.

"Isn't it beautiful?"

Behind him, just beyond the altar, a shadow wavered. A doorway appeared, a flickering fissure emerging from the darkness. Beyond the doorway, an even greater darkness, shrouded in fog. The fog spilled into the sanctuary, along with a chilling wind that swirled around Killian and Bennett, threatening the candle flames.

A new sound emerged, a faint roar. The roar became a thousand demonic screams, growing louder and louder. Tendrils of black smoke cut through the fog, reaching into the chapel, snakes testing the air on the other side.

"Holy water!" Bennett yelled. Killian stood slack-jawed, frozen in horror. "Killian! Holy water!"

Killian couldn't move. The doorway kept growing, its borders solidifying. A dark shadow, tall, foreboding, moved beyond the threshold, growing larger as it approached them. The overhead lights exploded, showering glass onto them.

"Killian! Holy water! Now!" Killian finally snapped out of it, racing to a marble pedestal near the entrance. Bennett advanced on Steven, his crucifix held high. "Begone you fiend, you vile abomination! Begone!"

Killian sprinted back, holding a bowl of holy water in both hands, trying not to spill it. Bennett ripped it from his arms. "Unplug everything! Break the boundary of the candles!"

Killian sprinted around the altar, unplugging the turntables. It did nothing. The records kept spinning, kept playing, spiraling faster and faster, the screams louder and louder.

Bennett tossed the holy water on Steven, and he reeled back, his skin blistering, melting away. "Begone, you children of Satan!"

Killian yanked up each needle, breaking off the turntable arms. He slammed two of the records onto the floor, shattering them. He did the same to the 8-track players, shoving them off the altar.

"No!" Steven screamed. He lunged forward, grabbing the last record before Killian could reach it. "Stay back!"

The sudden silence in the room was deafening. The doorway began to flicker and fade. The shrieks from the other side grew quiet. The looming shadow shrank back, pulling the smoky tendrils with it.

Bennett took a step forward. "Steven, it's me, it's okay. It's over."

Steven broke down in pained sobs. Bennett placed a hand on his shoulder. Steven's face was pockmarked with burns. One eye was gone, burst by the blessed water, its milky fluid streaming down his blackened cheek. Steven finally looked up, staring at Bennett, then Killian. He seemed to be himself again, just for a moment, before the twisted smile returned.

"You must hear them now..."

Steven smashed the record on the altar and shoved a jagged shard deep into Bennett's chest.

"No!" Killian yelled, lunging forward. It was too late. The narrow tip had slipped through Bennett's ribs, piercing his heart.

Bennett dropped to the floor. Steven raised the vinyl shard high in the air, blood streaming down his arm.

"Aren't they beautiful?" Steven asked. He was looking beyond Killian, at the corner of the ceiling, as if he was watching something move across it.

Killian scanned the empty sanctuary. "Who?"

"The triplets. Can't you see them? Can't you hear them?"

Steven buried the vinyl shard in his neck, slicing open his own throat. He collapsed to the ground, blood spurting from the serrated wound.

Killian gripped Bennett by the shoulders and pulled him towards the outer wall. Killian sat on the floor, Bennett between his legs. Bennett coughed, blood oozing from his mouth. The doorway behind the altar had disappeared completely. Only a few candles remained lit, their shadows dancing on the walls.

"I'm sorry," Bennett choked.

"Don't talk." Killian pressed his hand on Bennett's wound. Blood poured through his fingers, pooling on the floor around them.

"But I must. There are things you need to know. I'm sorry, Killian, but it's your burden now." Bennett loosened his collar, drawing out a gold chain. An ornate, antique key hung from the end. "We must be quick. I don't have much time."

Side A: Track 1:
Nina in the Motor City
(4:36)

1.

A record spun on one of two Technics 1200 turntables inside Nina's cramped, one-bedroom apartment. She worked the record with her hands, an obscure sixties R & B single she had unearthed the previous day. She had found it at the bottom of a dusty box, long neglected in the basement of a recently deceased woman from Brush Park. Nina scratched the record back and forth, manipulating a fragment of the drums. The turntable, a 1997 model, was connected to a Numark mixer from 1993, which served as the hub for several keyboards, a drum machine, and an AKAI sampler of similar vintage.

All of Nina's equipment was pre-2000, and this was by choice, not economics. Not that she would have been able to afford any new gear if she wanted it. She was one of the few twenty-five-year-olds in the world with an extreme aversion to modern technology. Even as a child she had gravitated towards all things analog, old radios, cassette players, VHS tapes.

She loved the simplicity older tech offered. It either worked, or it didn't, and if it didn't, she could usually fix it herself. There were no software updates, viruses, or system crashes to hold her back. Her cell phone, which she only purchased after years of relentless mocking from friends and family, was many years and several models behind, a cheap flip-phone with a cracked screen that could text, and not much else. That was just fine with her. Nina was generally happiest at home, with the rest of the world out of reach, and out of touch.

Nina lived alone amongst her production equipment and her children, her babies, her precious record collection. Nina's peeling walls were lined with cinder blocks and sagging DIY plywood shelves, filled with over ten thousand vinyl records. All genres and decades were represented in her obsessive crate-digging, which had been her main hobby since she was 13 years old.

She worked her sampler, replaying the fragment of drums over and over. Nina slowly molded the sound, transforming it into a lush hip-hop beat. It had been a good morning for making beats, and good mornings had been hard to come by lately. It wasn't always easy. Sometimes it was a real struggle for Nina to wake up, sit down, and create something, especially something good. But when she could, like today, the world would melt away, her anxieties flowing out of her body, replaced by a sense of euphoria.

Nina became laser-focused in these sessions, methodical, in her zone. Hours and hours would go by before she realized she was starving, her bladder bursting. That's what made the hunt worth it. All that time, flipping through dusty stacks of records in the basement of a random record shop or an off-the-beaten path antique store. When she found something like this, that no one else had claimed yet, and she made it her own? That was the definition of heaven for Nina.

Nina's cell phone buzzed. She opened it and glanced at the screen. Her father was calling. "Shit," she muttered to herself. She sent him to voicemail and went back to work.

2.

Nina made her way through an aging Detroit neighborhood on foot, juggling two large coffees. She passed a mix of business and older homes. Some businesses were closed, some homes were abandoned, boarded up. Others were hanging on, fresh paint and newly planted gardens, mom and pop businesses struggling to survive, fighting against the tide of gentrification. Nina had been born and raised in the heart of the city. She had only left the confines of the city limits a handful of times in her life, and she was just fine with that. There was no place on earth she would rather be.

Nina jogged across the street between two cars. Her father's store was located on the corner of a once-busy intersection, across from a laundromat and a small grocery store. Housed in the corner of a nondescript red-brick building, Round-A-Bout Reggie's record shop had been a staple of the local music scene for decades, even if you might miss the place walking by it for the first time.

The dusty, unwashed windows were covered in old newspapers to block out the damaging effects of the sun. Nina had long wanted to replace the newspapers with new, tinted windows, but the money wasn't there, at least, according to her dad. Only a small metal sign hung over the door, the store's name in a half-circle, hugging a cartoonish vinyl record.

Her father had wanted to update the logo, change the name, but Nina wouldn't have it. It had long passed the point of being dated, becoming perfectly retro in all the right ways. She wanted to put it on T-shirts and hats, but again, her father wouldn't spring for the investment required. Even though he was well known locally, they were often at odds over his store's reputation. Nina was endlessly frustrated with her father's lack of vision for it. He seemed happy to just let it slowly slide into obscurity, its many unearthed treasures left to gather dust and decay.

Nina carefully turned the doorknob, a coffee still in each hand, and slipped through the front door, the bell dinging as she entered. The store was a cavern inside, a maze of over one hundred thousand used vinyl records. Some were in bins, some were sorted in aisles, others were piled in the corners, towering towards the ceiling, only accessible via a ladder. It was an inventory that only the store's namesake could make any sense of. Reggie knew every square inch of it. If he had a record you wanted in his stock, he could find it. It might just take a few minutes, or a few hours.

Reggie stood behind the counter, a small gut dipping over his belt, and despite his sixty-five years of age, a full head of dark hair. Behind him, several decades of concert posters plastered the walls, many layers thick, their corners curling and yellowing. He beamed at the sight of his only daughter. "Ahh, she emerges from her cave!"

"Sorry, dad. Peace offering?" Nina joined him behind the counter, handing him a coffee.

"Sugar?" Reggie asked.

"Enough to kill ya."

"Perfect." Reggie took a big gulp, savoring it.

"Did you go?"

"You know I went, Nina. I go every Saturday. And you know that *I know* you blow me off every Saturday."

"I had that gig Friday night, the wedding. It went late."

"How was it?"

"Fourteen dollars in tips, and they asked me to play the Macarena three times."

Reggie howled at this. "Oh, shit."

"It's not funny! Maybe if I made a little more working here?"

"Ha! I pay you a fair wage, you just pay most of if back to me!"

"There might be some truth to that."

"Oh, you think?"

"Just a kernel."

Reggie chuckled again. "I have officially passed my addiction on to my daughter, and I couldn't be prouder." Reggie placed an arm around Nina's shoulder and pulled her in for a one-armed hug. "Seriously though. You really should join me one of these weekends."

"I know, dad, I know. It's just, cemeteries, all that, it creeps me out."

"It'd be good for you, all the same. Your mother would appreciate it."

"Okay, okay. Next week?"

"Deal." Reggie gave Nina a kiss on top of her head. "Now get to work. Another estate sale came in. Looks like we've got some real gems in there."

"Hell yeah!"

"Some gems *to sell*. Not to squirrel away for yourself."

"Yeah, yeah." Nina pulled herself away, laughing, and rolled up her sleeves.

3.

It ended up being a busy day in the shop. Several regulars came in and found what they were looking for, and an eccentric tourist from Germany dropped $500 on some pristine Motown 45s. Large sales like that always gave Nina a sense of relief, even if only temporary. If they could get a few more of those, it wouldn't be a bad month. They might even make a tiny profit after paying their mounting bills.

By 8:00, Nina was wrapping up. She swept the floor, emptied the trash, and wiped down the bathroom before calling it a day. Reggie was at the till sorting receipts. Nina approached him sheepishly, a dozen records in hand. That estate sale had indeed held some hidden gems. He saw the stack and rolled his eyes.

"Let me take a look," Reggie grumbled, flipping through the pile.

"There's nothing of value in there, dad. Everything worth any money has been priced and stocked on the floor."

Satisfied, Reggie gave the records back. "Good work today."

"You good, dad? Mind if I head out?"

"Yep, I might leave the light on for another hour, then I'm calling it. Any big plans tonight?"

Nina held up her new finds. "Just this."

Reggie shook his head, "When am I going to hear something you've made?"

Nina broke eye contact. "When it's good enough."

"How do you know if it's any good if you never let anyone hear it?"

"You sound like Maggie."

"How is Maggie, by the way? You ever hear from her?" Reggie asked.

Nina immediately regretted saying her name, "No. And you know I don't like talking about it."

"Maggie was a keeper."

"Dad, I swear..."

"And she was a good cook."

"Dad!" Nina playfully punched her father in the shoulder before heading for the door. "Good night!"

"Breakfast tomorrow?" Reggie asked.

"Same time and place."

Nina opened the front door. Reggie called after her. "You should bring Maggie!"

Nina shook her head as she headed down the sidewalk. *What an asshole*, she chuckled to herself. Reggie had been completely supportive when Nina had come out a few years back, like she knew he would be. The rest of the extended family was a different story, but that was also not surprising. Her father had led a wild life outside of Detroit before finally landing back in the place of his birth.

Reggie had bounced around the east coast for a few years after high school in the late seventies, playing drums in various jazz fusion bands, before being drawn into faster, heavier music. He happened to land in DC during the foundation of their punk scene, and his career peaked with a slot opening for Bad Brains in 1981, dodging beer bottles from an unimpressed crowd.

Not long after Bad Brains relocated to New York City, Reggie made his way back to Detroit, and reconnected with his high school sweetheart, Nina's mother. There was very little photographic evidence of her father's punk years, and this pained Nina greatly. What she wouldn't give for some blackmail like that to hold over him.

Nina tried not to think of her ex, Maggie, but she was never far from her mind. Only after Maggie had left her could Nina admit to herself how much she had meant to her. Maggie was amazing, and as obsessed with music as Nina was. She had worked as a concert promoter for years in Detroit, before landing her dream gig as the first female, Asian-American radio DJ in the city, working for a local hip-hop station.

They had dated for nearly two years. It had been Nina's first serious relationship with a woman. Looking back now, Nina knew the break-up had been completely her fault. Nina had always kept her at a distance, her own insecurities around her music, and her life in general, clouding her judgement. Losing her mother to cancer hadn't helped things. Nina had been in a bad place all around, and Maggie became collateral damage.

Maggie leaving her had been a wakeup call. With her father's urging, and his financial help, Nina had started therapy, going once a week. It was hard, but she was slowly figuring her shit out, finding herself in a better place. She still thought about Maggie almost daily and had countless drafts of unsent texts to her. Her therapist wanted her to delete them, but Nina couldn't, not yet at least.

Side A: Track 2: A Man Down (3:52)

1.

James Dewitt, a.k.a. ManDown, slipped inside Round-A-Bout Reggie's door, locking it behind him. He flipped the window sign to 'Closed.' ManDown was dressed in all black. Black sneakers, black jeans, and a black hoodie, which he always wore up, covering his face in shadow. He carried a black messenger bag, a retro child's portable turntable, and a six-pack of beer. He scanned the inside of the store, nervous.

Reggie laughed, "Don't worry, you're the only person in here."

"I thought she'd never leave."

"She's a good kid, hard worker."

ManDown shook Reggie's hand, gave him a beer, "I appreciate the discretion."

"Your secret's always safe with me. How's the album coming?"

"It's not," ManDown replied.

"Sorry to hear that."

"Should never have signed with a major."

"They get you with that briefcase full of shiny bills, don't they? Well, maybe this will help."

Reggie bent down, searching through a crate behind the counter. He pulled out an ultra-rare 45 rpm single, an obscure Japanese release from the sixties. "This came in the other day. Thought you might dig it. Pretty sure no one's ever sampled this shit."

ManDown poured over the cover, the production credits on the back, "Can't believe your daughter didn't cop this one."

"I never let her lay eyes on it. I still need to make a living."

Reggie was one of the only people on earth who knew the real identity of the music producer known as ManDown. Not even Nina knew that he was a regular customer. Reggie dreaded the day she might find out. ManDown had been an early influence on her beat-making. Reggie could only imagine the expletives that would be rained down upon him if she found out he knew him all these years.

It was one of the reasons Reggie kept pushing his daughter to let him hear her music. He had a feeling it was much better than she let on, and if he could get it in the hands of someone like ManDown, who knows? A co-sign by him would be huge for her career, and ManDown owed Reggie at least that much.

Reggie had known ManDown since he was a child. His mother and Reggie's wife were old friends. When Reggie first met him, he was a scrawny, ultra-sensitive, super-shy piano-playing prodigy. His introversion and anxieties worsened during his teenage years, and he eventually dropped out of high school, got kicked out of his house, and even spent a summer sleeping in the basement of Reggie's store.

It was during that summer, living in a dark musty cave built of vinyl records, that James became reborn as ManDown. He re-emerged with a new identity, and a renewed focus in music. Reggie didn't understand the alter-ego at first, but it gave him the confidence he had always lacked. Hiding behind a mask, a veil of obscurity, made him stronger as a person and as an artist. They maintained a relationship over the years, even after his career exploded. Occasionally, when ManDown was seeking inspiration, he would text Reggie, and Reggie would keep the store open just for him.

A few hours later, ManDown was still digging through records as Reggie worked behind the counter doing paperwork. Reggie sipped a beer while smoking a joint, a jazz record playing on the speakers. ManDown had a huge stack of vinyl already pulled. He would place a record on his portable turntable, moving the needle, skimming each track, searching for breaks, listening for good samples.

"You really sold a first pressing of 'Kind of Blue'?" ManDown asked.

Reggie took a drag, nodding, "I did."

"How much?"

"You don't want to know."

ManDown joined Reggie at the counter. He took a hit off the joint, grabbed another beer from the nearly empty six-pack, "C'mon. How much?"

"Hundred bucks."

"What? That's a fucking tragedy. Miles is not looking down on you kindly."

"Shit. Miles rolls over in his grave every time you kids chop up his records."

"Hey now."

"You don't remember the lean years, son. Everyone buying CDs, no online sales yet. I almost didn't make it. Vinyl wasn't a fad with you kids then, like it is now."

ManDown grimaced at the accusation, "Records aren't a fad for me, man. I'm an artist. I make real music."

Reggie chuckled. "Whatever you say. I'm not sure I'd call it music, but I appreciate your patronage all the same."

ManDown handed the joint back to Reggie. "Now, I've been coming into your store for damn near twenty years now. And I buy stacks of records every time, right?"

Reggie frowned, unsure where this was going. "You want a medal or something?"

"I know you're holding out on me. Where is your *real* collection?"

Reggie's friendly demeanor disappeared. "What are you talking about?"

"I know you have some true rarities. I see the shit Nina sells online, and I've never seen anything in this store worth more than ten bucks. Where's the rest of your 'Kind of Blues'? I've got real money now, you know?"

Reggie threw up his hands, "What you see is what I got. This is everything."

ManDown pointed to a door in the back corner of the store. "Can I hit up your basement? I seem to remember quite a few locked doors down there back in the day. Let me see, I'll pay top dollar. My head's been against a wall for months." He pointed at the Japanese 45. "I need more of that. My album needs it. I'm way past deadline, and I need to come out swinging, blow people's minds."

"I wish I could help son; I really do," Reggie checked his watch without really checking it. "I think it's time I close up for the night."

"What, already?"

"I'm getting old! I need my beauty sleep."

"C'mon, I was just messing with you. Can I buy you a burger at least, let me hear some more Round-A-Bout Reggie music biz war stories?"

"Not tonight." Reggie stubbed out the roach in a glass ashtray.

2.

ManDown stood across the street from Reggie's store, hidden in the shadows of an alleyway. He checked his watch; it was just after midnight. Above the store, a light was on, a small apartment on the second floor. Through the window, he could see Reggie in bed, reading a book. He finally closed it, set it on his nightstand, and turned out the light.

ManDown jogged across the street, and made his way down the opposite alley, circling around to the back of the building. He pulled a crowbar from his bag, gently sliding it into the crack of the rear door. He wiggled the crowbar back and forth slowly, gently splintering the wood. The lock popped off suddenly, and loudly, clattering across the pavement. ManDown jumped back, scanning the second floor for lights. All was still quiet and dark. Behind him, a stray dog trotted past, growling as he embarked on his nightly hunt.

ManDown tip-toed down creaky wooden steps, his cellphone lighting his way. The basement was dark, dank, unfinished. A sea of dusty vinyl records waited for him. Tens of thousands of them, lining the walls, the floor. He pulled a string attached to a bare bulb. Water dripped from a pipe in the ceiling. A rat scurried by. He looked around in disbelief. The place had deteriorated considerably since he had last seen it.

ManDown made his way deeper into the bowels of the basement. The stacks of records got older and more unorganized the farther back he made it. Some were waterlogged, warped, others eaten by moths and rats. Against the back wall was a locked metal door. He remembered it from when he was a kid, it had always been locked then as well.

As he moved closer to the door, a darkness grew in his mind, clouding his vision, pushing out his own thoughts. He stopped, turning around, searching the basement behind him with his light. He could have sworn he heard someone whispering. After confirming he was alone, he focused on the padlock, which he easily popped off with the crowbar.

ManDown flipped a switch and found himself transported into an immaculate, mid-century listening lounge, complete with walnut wood paneling, an orange shag rug, and globe lamps flecked with gold. In one corner was a fully stocked bar, all bamboo and wicker, next to a vintage, striped recliner. Next to that were several crates of records, and a high-end turntable.

ManDown flipped through the crates, a collection of mint-condition collector's items and imported rarities. He felt a pang of guilt, betraying Reggie's trust like this, but he was desperate. He knew the old man had been holding out on him, and he was right. These crates proved it. The lights flickered twice, and ManDown wheeled around, his heart pounding. No one was there. Next to the door was a single shelf. The wooden shelf only held one item, a thick glass case, which housed a single record. Its jacket was blank, only a matte-black finish.

At that moment, everything else in the world disappeared. Whatever that jacket contained, ManDown needed it. It called out to him, pulling him into its poisonous orbit. ManDown made his way to the shelf on rubbery legs, adrenaline coursing through his veins. He opened the glass case carefully, the lights flickering again.

ManDown took a step back, wincing, rubbing his temples, a sudden headache spreading within his skull. The record was *loud*, just sitting on a shelf. A deep bass throbbed in his ears, so forcefully they plugged up. He took the record out of the case and carefully slipped the vinyl out of its jacket. It was an antique. A thick, acetate, 78 rpm record, its center label crimson red, the number one stenciled on it in ornate calligraphy. He placed it gently on the turntable and clamped Reggie's headphones over his ears.

3.

Reggie woke with a start. His head was pounding, his breath escaping him. He had dreamed of the record beneath him, spinning at that very moment, for the first time in over a decade. He knew immediately something was wrong, he could feel it in his bones. Catching his breath, he grabbed a baseball bat and headed downstairs.

Just as he feared, his back door was standing ajar. He tip-toed down the basement steps slowly, allowing his eyes time to adjust to the dark. He could see a sliver of light spilling from his lounge as he approached it. He stopped before the half-closed door, holding the bat tight in front of his chest.

"Hello? Who's in there?" There was no reply. "I mean no harm, I won't call the cops, I just want you to leave, alright?"

Still nothing.

Reggie crept forward, pushing the door open with the tip of the bat. ManDown stood in the corner, facing the wall. Headphones still on, his head bobbed slowly up and down. The record was over, the needle scraping the dead wax, rubbing against the inner label.

"What the hell are you doing?" Reggie yelled.

ManDown yanked off the headphones, throwing them onto the floor. The cord unplugged from the receiver, and a crackling static poured through the speakers, filling the air, deafening inside the small room. Beneath the static, children whispered, laughing, speaking in an unintelligible language.

Reggie stepped towards him. "Turn that off, man!"

ManDown slowly turned around, a grim smile spreading across his face. "You've been holding out on me, Reggie." Flames burned faintly behind ManDown's eyes.

Reggie shook his head, "What have you done, kid?"

"Do you hear them?"

Reggie raised the bat and lunged at the turntable, aiming for the record. ManDown jumped between Reggie and his target, catching the bat with one hand. ManDown shoved Reggie back, slamming him into the wall. The bat slipped from Reggie's hand as he hit the floor. His shoulder was dislocated, he rubbed it, in pain.

"James, man, please! You don't know what that is!"

ManDown picked up the bat. The static grew louder and louder, shrieking out of the speakers. Reggie pulled himself to his knees, staring up at ManDown.

"Turn it off! Please! Unplug everything, for the love of God!"

ManDown raised the bat over his head and brought it down repeatedly, with all the strength he had. Reggie's skull splintered from the blows, his body crumpling to the floor. The record sped up, spinning faster and faster as Reggie's blood spattered the grooves, the static growing even louder as ManDown pummeled Reggie's lifeless body.

4.

ManDown stepped into the street in front of the store, bathed in the moonlight, a reborn man once again. He breathed in the night air, tasting a new world, his senses heightened, his nerves on fire. He could feel the record, inside his messenger bag, throbbing with power, with infinite possibilities. He knew his journey had finally come to an end. He had what he needed, the final, missing piece. His album would soon be completed, and it would be his masterpiece.

He darted across the street, ducking into the shadows of the alley on the other side. He placed his bag on the ground and removed several cans of spray paint. It was time to let the world know. ManDown was back.

Side A: Track 3: The Triplets Re-Awaken (3:34)

1.

Nina sat at their usual booth, waiting for her father. The diner, an old-school mom-and-pop neighborhood institution, was slammed, as it had been since it first opened in the fifties. It had been Nina's favorite place to eat for as long as she could remember. Her first time there, Nina's head had barely reached the tabletop. She loved the red vinyl booths, the long lunch counter, and most of all, the mammoth plates of hot and greasy food.

Nina and her father met at the diner weekly, ever since her mom died. It was a routine Reggie had started in part to make sure they maintained a healthy relationship outside of work. No shop talk was allowed inside the diner, a rule that he strictly enforced. Nina had been apprehensive at first, because she knew the conversation would inevitably lead to her mother, but the breakfasts became beneficial to them both, an informal therapy session that Nina looked forward to more and more each week.

Nina checked her watch again. Her father was really late now, over thirty minutes. She was worried. She tried his cell again, but it went to voicemail. His regular order, an omelet with extra feta cheese, sat cooling across from her half-eaten French toast.

Diane, the owner, swung by the booth, refilling coffee mugs. "You want me to box that up for the old man?"

"Yeah, I guess. Looks like I got stood up."

Diane frowned. "That's not like Reggie."

"No, it's not. Not at all."

Nina paid the bill and hurried out the door. She knew in her gut something was very wrong.

2.

Nina shoved her key into the front door of the shop, but it swung inward, already open and unlocked. The shop was dark inside, empty. Nina set the to-go box on the counter. "I'm sorry I didn't make it on Saturday, but that's no reason to take it out on your number four with extra cheese!" The building was eerily quiet. She noticed the basement door was open, a light on.

She reluctantly went down the steps. She hated the store's basement. She'd feared it ever since she was a child, and her dad would tease her about the monsters hiding in its corners. She knew there were no monsters now, but she'd seen enough creepy-crawlies down there that she avoided it at all costs.

Nina stepped around the piles of records. The lack of organization drove her crazy. Everything needed to be catalogued, alphabetized.

Who knew what unknown gems lay hidden amongst the trash? She had long ago given up on her father ever tackling it, and she sure as hell wasn't going to crawl around down there on her hands and knees.

"Dad? You down here?"

That was when she noticed the open door, a yellowish light spilling out. *The* door, to *the room*. The one place that had always been off limits to her, her entire life. Once, when she was ten, her father had left the padlock unlatched. She had only made it two steps inside the room when he came rushing down the stairs, yanking her out by her arm. She remembered little of what she saw, just a single record on a high shelf.

It was the first and only time in her life that he'd laid hands on her, spanking her over his knee. He felt so bad afterwards that he immediately took her out for ice cream. Nina was pretty sure he had shed more tears than she had over the whole thing, but it worked. She never asked him about it again, never tried to find the key. She just let it go, even as an adult.

Her heart racing, she stepped across the threshold. She had no idea what she was walking into. A fantastic listening lounge was the last thing she had expected. Why had he kept this from her? She assumed she'd find a stack of Playboys and an old Lazy-Boy, or something equally gross, but this?

Then she saw him, her father, slumped in the corner. He was beaten so badly; she wouldn't have recognized him if it wasn't for his clothes. His prized records were smashed, littered across the floor, along with the turntable and speakers. She raced to him, even though she knew he had to be dead.

"Dad?" She felt for a pulse. His skin was cold and hard, the blood already dried brown. She collapsed, her hands gripping his shoulders, "No, no, no, no..."

3.

The sun blinded Nina as she stumbled out of the store, her hands and shirt covered in blood. Sobbing uncontrollably, she leaned over, vomiting onto the street. Across the road, a small crowd was forming. Hip-hop heads in their late teens and early twenties, all with their phones out, taking selfies, posting live on their feeds, talking excitedly amongst themselves.

Nina crossed the street, a grief-induced trance, and the crowd grew quiet at the sight of her, wobbling slowly towards them, covered in her father's blood. The throng parted for her, aiming their phones at her now. She stood before a brick wall in the alley, which was covered in a massive mural.

It was an *incredible* piece of art, dark and foreboding. A ghost-like specter, ten feet tall, floated behind two massive turntables and a mixer. Blood oozed from the apparition's fingers, running over the turntables, down the brick wall. The spray-painted blood appeared to pool on the tar below it, forming a large puddle. The puddle spelled out the words:

'Symphony of Screams – VOL: III – Coming Soon.'

A college kid stepped forward, snapping photos. "He's back. ManDown's back!"

Nina collapsed to her knees, on the verge of passing out. The kid rushed to her side to steady her. "Hey, you okay?"

4.

Five miles away, a small house stood on a once vibrant corner. Like many houses in the neighborhood, it had seen better days. Its paint was peeling, the roof needed new shingles, a shutter was hanging on by one last rusty nail, flapping in the breeze.

Unlike the other houses in the neighborhood, its mortgage was paid in full, its taxes were paid two years out, and it was equipped with a state-of-the-art security system. The tiny camera on the porch was barely visible to the naked eye. You could only hear its vibrating hum if you were standing on the front steps, directly beneath it. The neighbors didn't pay the house any mind. People rarely went in and out, and there was never any trouble there, no parties, no loud music, no broken-down cars rusting on the lawn.

The backyard was surrounded by a faded six-foot high wooden fence. The grass within it was spotty, overgrown, strangled by weeds. In the center of the yard, a steel hatch protruded from the soil. Only visible if you were standing directly over it, it was the entrance to a Cold-War era underground bunker.

This bunker served as ManDown's production studio. A ladder led down to an enormous room, its walls made of crumbling, water-stained cement. Every square foot of wall space was covered with metal racks, sagging with tens of thousands of records. There was a cot in the corner, next to a mini-fridge and a microwave. ManDown slept there most nights.

His childhood home had felt less and less like his own in the years since his mother had passed. He only used it to shower, and when he needed food he would spend an anxious hour in the living room, waiting for it to be delivered. Otherwise, the bunker was his domain.

ManDown sat before a vast array of monitors, laptops, turntables, keyboards, samplers, and drum machines. He wasn't sure how long he'd been sitting there, or what the time was. He had only a vague recollection of the previous night, and no idea how he had gotten home.

His mind was no longer completely his own. He was still its main occupant, but a small piece of the darkness locked inside the record had broken in, joining him. A tiny sliver of malignancy squatting in the depths of his consciousness. That darkness was growing, metastasizing, wading through his thoughts and emotions, studying his weaknesses. He knew it wanted complete control.

The stolen record spun on his vintage 78 RPM turntable, still sticky with Reggie's blood. Over the static, an old man's voice spilled out of the speakers, faint, scratchy. *"And who do you three claim to be?"* He was answered by three voices, children, girls, all overlapping, their tones swinging from impossibly high pitches to deep bass growls, speaking in an indecipherable tongue. The language gave way to laughter, the children cackling in ragged breaths.

ManDown adjusted levels on his immense mixing board. He was recording the record as it played, transferring it to his hard drive. He queued it up, dropping the MP3 into a channel on his monitor. He played the recording back, layering it on top of the vinyl. He copied it again, adding another channel, playing it over itself a third time, adjusting the speed of each channel, chopping up the audio, the children's voices becoming a thick wall of static and moans.

The lights above him flickered and went off, plunging him into darkness. He slid back his chair, ready to stumble his way to the fuse box. He often pushed the aging circuitry past its limit. He froze. He could feel something in the room with him. A presence, behind him in the dark. The hairs on his arms rose, his skin crawled. He swiveled around, peering into the blackness.

"Hello?"

Something rushed towards him. He could feel the change in the air, a sucking sound as it got closer. He twisted back to his desk, fumbling for a flashlight. Something clamped down on his shoulder; a sharp pain, he screamed in terror.

The lights popped back on, and ManDown was alone in his bunker. He bolted up, scanning the room, clawing at his back. He sprinted to a mirror on the wall, yanking down his shirt. There was a bite mark just below his neck. Small, neat, as if a child had attempted to make a meal out of him. "What the fuck?" He muttered to himself.

The turntable started up on its own behind him, filling the room with loud static. Underneath the static, the children laughed, as if mocking him. Their voices finally came together, all three speaking at once, with authority.

"Aperi lanuam."

ManDown leaped towards the turntable, yanking the needle off the record. The lights flickered again, and dimmed, leaving him in near darkness. The room was silent, and for the first time in his bunker, ManDown felt claustrophobic. He headed for the ladder; it was time for some fresh air. A breeze hit his back. He spun around, facing the shadows, squinting in the dim light. "Hello?"

The darkness answered him, shattering his eardrums, "Aperi lanuam!"

A tendril of shadow and smoke shot out of the darkness, attacking him like a coiled snake. The smoke poured into his mouth, his nose, his ears, overwhelming his body. ManDown howled in pain. The lights above him exploded, showering him in glass, leaving him in darkness, curled up in a ball on the cement floor.

The only light came from his eyes, yellow embers, glowing in the dark.

Side A: Interlude 1: The Man, the Myth (1:34)

The following is an excerpt from the unfinished feature-length documentary, *'The Man, the Myth: Who is ManDown?'* produced by Jacob Friedman. It was set to be an expansion of his thesis project, an award-winning short he directed while a student at NYU. Despite going heavily into debt producing it and securing interviews with a who's who of hip-hop royalty, Mr. Friedman eventually abandoned the project, leaving it unfinished and unreleased after its subject repeatedly refused to be interviewed. In fact, Mr. Friedman was never able to prove that his subject even existed.

FADE IN:

<u>DJ MUGGS</u> - ManDown? What can you say about ManDown? He's a legend, one of the best crate diggers ever...

HAVOC - I always felt a kinship with him, you know? Even though he was out of Detroit, at least, *I* think he's from Detroit. We had similar upbringings, similar struggles...

EL-P - He's up there with Dilla for sure. His mixtape run, The Scrolls? Legendary...

DJ MUGGS - I'm digging for records constantly; I have literally tens of thousands of records. There are samples ManDown uses, I mean, no one knows where they came from...

HAVOC – And he was one of the few younger producers with a truly encyclopedic knowledge of the golden era of hip-hop...

EL-P - He wasn't just a mimic though, you know, doing some tired throwback sound, parroting the Boom-Bap years. He was elevating the art form. And his skills with paint? I mean, it's way beyond tagging, he's up there with Banksy. True street art...

DJ MUGGS - Like a lot of us, he started with funk and soul samples, but his appetite grew, like it does in the greats. Then things got real dark, you know? Choral samples, strings, sinister organs. His last mixtape, Scrolls Volume Two? I know an MC, who shall remain nameless, who claimed that album made him physically nauseous. Like, he literally can't listen to that shit any more...

HAVOC - We were all waiting on Scrolls Volume Three, the whole industry, and then, well, you know.

JACOB (O.S.) - Pretend I don't. What happened?

HAVOC - Well, that's just it. Nobody knows. He just disappeared. Poof, gone. No one has seen or heard from him in what, two years now?

EL-P - There are crazy stories, for sure. People claiming he's living in France, or dead.

JACOB (O.S.) - Do you think that? That he's dead?

EL-P - No. No way. There are sightings, every once in a while. Always a grainy photo you can't quite make out though, like he's fucking Sasquatch or something...

DJ MUGGS - No, I like to think he's out there somewhere, underground, perfecting Volume three. Maybe on some serious Howard Hughes shit by now, but, you know...

HAVOC - He's out there. He has to be. He'll re-emerge when he's ready, hit us with another masterpiece...

FADE TO BLACK

{flip the record}

Side B: Track 1: Bloody Dreams and Bleeding Scars (3:21)

1.

Killian Connolly slept behind a massive mahogany desk, snoring softly. His clerical collar was unclasped, half falling out of his shirt, his shoeless feet resting on his desk. This had become a bad habit for him after lunch. He worked mostly alone, and rarely had visitors, so his afternoons had turned into extended siestas as of late.

This afternoon was different. Killian dreamed of that fateful night in 1975 for the first time in decades. His roommate's throat gushing blood; his mentor bleeding out in his arms; the flickering candles, the spinning records, the terrible darkness hovering just beyond the threshold of our world. He had run from it all in the dream, but the chapel doors had been locked, covered in thick, steel chains. He banged on the doors, screaming for help. Behind him, the shadow grew, and a darkness raced forward, consuming him.

A crow smashed against the stained-glass window above him, cracking a crimson panel. Killian awoke with a start, spilling a ceramic mug of cold coffee across his desk. He felt a sharp pain in his cheek. He touched his weathered scar with a napkin, a few drops of blood beaded on the cheap paper, forming a small circle. Killian's stomach constricted, and his large office suddenly felt very small, and very hot. He needed some fresh air.

2.

Killian sauntered across the commons of St. John's, a campus he had never really left after that ill-fated night. He sat at his favorite bench; a place still haunted by the ghost of what could have been. Killian watched the dying leaves swirl along the path in front of him. He rubbed his scar again; it was tight, tender. He hadn't noticed its presence on his face since the eighties. It had fully healed long ago, becoming a part of him he rarely even noticed in a mirror.

But Killian had felt something was off the last few weeks, a subtle change deep inside of him. He brushed it off as the coming of old age, and the melancholy that accompanies that inescapable transition, but on some level, he knew it was more sinister than that. The dream only confirmed his suspicions, along with the blood currently seeping from his face.

In the distance, the library building loomed over the commons, casting a long shadow across the lawn. A massive flock of crows swirled above it. A few began to divebomb the peaked roof. When Killian squinted, he could already see a half-dozen black bodies littering the gables. Killian grimaced as he rose, his knees and right hip cracking.

He had inherited arthritis from his mother, and the crisp fall air did it no favors.

As he made his way to the library, Killian realized he was following a long line of ants along the sidewalk. Thousands of them were marching towards the building with him, crawling in and out of the cracks in the cement. He examined the perimeter of the library. The soil along the granite foundation was teeming with nightcrawlers, writhing on the surface, a frenzied orgy. A few attempted to scale the slick stone.

The first story windows were similarly invaded, swarms of black beetles pressing against the glass, trying to find a way inside. Several dead crows lay in the grass, their bodies falling from the slanted roof after diving to their deaths. Swarms of flies fought a vicious war for real estate on their decaying bodies.

3.

Killian made his way through the massive, multi-level library. It was the pride of the university, the entire Catholic church for that matter, one of the largest of its kind outside of Europe. It was all marble tile and dark wood, countless rows of books rising towards a cathedral-like peak with massive oak beams crisscrossing the ceiling. Scattered throughout the main level, lit glass cases housed brittle scrolls, jewel-encrusted chalices, and other ancient Christian artifacts.

Killian had been the head curator of the library and archives for several decades. He would occasionally teach a class on biblical archeology, but he much preferred to be behind the scenes, or "hiding in the shadows," as his colleagues often joked. Killian poured himself into his work, acquiring and saving sacred texts from all over the world. He was proud of the collection he had helped amass, even if he wouldn't admit it out loud.

Killian reached the back of the library. A dark corner filled with outdated books gathering dust. Books current students rarely requested. His suspicions were confirmed. The line of ants continued all the way through the library, hiding within the dark, chipped grout of the marble floor. The ants approached the wall of books before him, one after another, and disappeared beneath it.

Killian slid a book to the side and yanked on the shelf, pulling it out. It swung forward on hidden wheels. Behind it was a large antique door, made of dark, varnished wood. A lattice of black metal adorned it, long vines meeting in the center, framing a large cross. Killian reached into his shirt, removing the ornate key gifted to him by Professor Bennett before his death.

This was the reason he had never really left St. John's, the reason he had turned his back on so many potential paths in his young life. The reason he was still a priest, even though his faith in a just God had died that night in 1975.

4.

Killian slid the key into an intricate locking system at the center of the cross made of brass. He turned it slowly, listening to the aging gears squeaking behind the wood. He swung the door inward, and made his way inside, to the *real* archives. Unlike the rest of the library, there were no fancy display cases, no spotlights. This room served as a vault, a vault filled with rare and dangerous religious texts and artifacts. Killian was one of only a few men in the world who knew of its existence.

The novelty of that fact had long worn off on Killian, and he was only left with the burden of it all. A burden he knew he would have to pass on sooner rather than later. This was a cause of much anxiety for Killian. He would scan the fresh faces of the young seminarians each year, wondering who he might task with taking on such a responsibility. A responsibility that would shatter everything they thought they knew about the church and shake the foundations of their faith. There were some very dark secrets inside that room. Secrets that needed to be kept at all costs.

Killian followed the ants, already certain where they would lead him. One corner of the archives contained a wall of metal shelves, overflowing with reel-to-reel tapes and film canisters. Beneath them was a wooden crate, housing a set of vinyl records. The outer record was marked with a red label, and the number one. The line of ants ended there. Blood was sweating from the records, a pool of it on the floor. Thousands of ants swarmed the puddle, the floor, a line of them continuing up the shelving, the records themselves covered in a writhing mass.

The lights in the room flickered. Killian rubbed his cheek, another drop of blood oozed from his scar. He shook his head, his heart racing.

It was happening again.

Side B: Track 2: The Weight of Loss (5:32)

1.

The week after her father's death was a blur for Nina. She attempted to bury her grief by focusing on the funeral arrangements. This kept her busy during the day at least, struggling to write a fitting obituary, picking out flowers, choosing a casket, notifying friends, relatives, business associates. Only at night, alone in her bed, would the reality of everything come crashing down upon her.

Sleep would elude her, and she would sob into her pillow, wondering how to pay for everything. The suddenness of his death didn't help things. She didn't know if her father had a will, or how to get access to his accounts to figure out what he had for savings, if any. It seemed like a mountain of heartbreaking tasks loomed before her.

Luckily, her aunt Eloise, Reggie's oldest sister, stepped up and helped Nina through the emotional minefield laid at her feet. Eloise had experienced her fair share of tragedy in her own life, and she worked with Nina every day leading up to the memorial service, doing what she could to ease Nina's burden. Nina had no idea how to repay Eloise for her kindness.

It was a fitting day for a funeral. Cloudy, cool, the hint of winter on the horizon. Afterwards, the crowd slowly dispersed from the graveside. Nina had been adamant that the service be short and to the point. She knew her father wouldn't have wanted a long, drawn-out event with endless speeches and crying.

Eloise stood by Nina's side, her arm tight around Nina's shoulder. A long line of family, friends, and loyal customers passed them by, stopping to offer their condolences. The outpouring of love and kind words for her father was almost too much to take. Nina's legs felt physically weak. She wondered how long it had been since she had eaten something. Thankfully, the crowd began to thin out.

Eloise stared at Nina's parents' gravestones; a vase of fresh-cut flowers adorned her mother's grave. "A beautiful bouquet. She would love that you thought of her today too."

"That's actually from my dad. He brought her fresh flowers every week."

Eloise pulled her in even tighter for a hug. "Oh honey. You're too young to have lost them both." Nina could only cry into her shoulder in response. "You've still got me in your corner, okay? You're not alone in this."

"I wish I had your strength."

"It's the price you pay for living a long life. You eventually become the matriarch of your family, whether you want to be or not."

Nina dried her eyes with a tissue. Her aunt was peering into the distance, squinting. "Is that a friend of your father's?"

Nina followed her gaze. A hundred feet away, Killian Connolly stood in the shadow of a large oak tree. He was watching them, the crowd.

"Definitely not. Dad hasn't stepped foot in a church since mom's funeral."

Someone gently tapped Nina on the shoulder. She turned to find Maggie standing beside her, attempting a smile through tears.

"Oh my God!" Nina gave her a big hug. "Maggie! Thank you so much for coming." Nina separated, staring at her, still in disbelief. "Seriously. You have no idea how much this means to me." Nina embraced her again, sobbing.

Eloise gave them some space. Maggie slowly pulled away.

"Of course I came. I'm so sorry, Nina. Your dad was amazing. It's not right, what happened." Nina wiped her eyes. "I just wanted you to know that I'm thinking about you, and your family."

"Thank you."

"Do they have any idea who did it?"

"No. They think it's kids, a burglary gone wrong."

Maggie stared at the gravestones, shaking her head. "Jesus. That's horrible. I'm so sorry."

"Thank you, again, for coming. He always liked you. He'd be touched."

"I really liked him too, Nina."

They stood together, an awkward silence. Nina finally looked her in the eyes, "Hey, do you want to maybe grab coffee sometime? Catch up?"

It came out wrong, too eager, and Nina instantly regretted saying it.

Maggie studied her shoes. "I should really get to work. I just wanted to pay my respects. You take care of yourself, okay?"

Maggie squeezed Nina's shoulder before leaving. Nina stared at her longingly as she walked away. When she turned back to the oak tree, the priest hovering in its shadow was gone.

2.

The sun was setting behind Round-A-Bout Reggie's, casting an orange glow over the street. Nina, still in her funeral dress, took in the growing memorial outside her father's store. The sidewalk was littered with flowers, balloons, and homemade signs. *"We love you, Reggie!"*, *"One of the best to ever do it!"* Someone had even left a rare Motown 7-inch record in tribute. It was worth at least a hundred dollars, and the fact that it still sat there on the sidewalk untouched left Nina overcome with emotion yet again. It made her love her little niche community of weirdos more than ever.

Nina made a vow to herself right then and there to do whatever she could to ensure the future of the store, of her father's legacy. She owed it to everyone who called his store home, everyone who felt just a little less out of place there, digging through stacks of records with their own kind, unjudged, geeking out over all things music.

Nina heard squawking above her. She stepped off the sidewalk into the street. Two dozen crows flew in a circle above the building. Occasionally they crashed into one another, and a vicious mid-air fight ensued. She watched a pair of black feathers float down to her, coming to rest on the sidewalk. Their tips were bloody from the violence of their removal. The whole scene left her queasy. She felt like dying prey beneath circling vultures. She hurried inside.

3.

The silence inside Reggie's apartment unnerved Nina even more than the crows outside. This was a space that had always been filled with music and laughter, and the smells of her father's incredible cooking. Now it felt cold, sterile, like a tomb. Nina threw on a record, cranked it up loud, and turned on every light she could find. She stepped out of her ill-fitting dress as quickly as she could, replacing it with sweats and a t-shirt from her backpack. She couldn't remember that last time she had been in a dress. Probably her mother's funeral.

Her parent's apartment had gradually morphed into a hip bachelor pad after her mother's death. Not that her dad had ever entertained women there. He had sworn that he would never remarry after his wife died, and he had kept his word.

Her mom had only accommodated his vices to a point, forcing him to keep a large percentage of his prized possessions in boxes, rather than on display. After her death, the walls were slowly covered in vintage concert posters, and towering stacks of records. The plush furniture was gradually replaced with vintage pieces, the seventies era her father missed so much, and her mother's feminine touch had been gently erased from the apartment. Nina took it all in, staring at the contents of her father's life, and wondered where to begin. She decided to start with a beer.

Nina sat cross-legged on the floor, boxes and bins from her father's closet spread out before her. Eloise told her that going through his stuff could wait, but Nina knew that she needed to stay active, keep her mind occupied with busy work. It was better than thinking, which for Nina, would only lead to spiraling, and another sleepless night.

Nina leafed through a stack of yellowing photographs she'd found in a shoebox. Photos of her as a child, photos that perfectly captured her total-nerd phase, all scrawny limbs and coke bottle glasses. Nina wiped tears from her cheeks and finished her beer.

It was dark outside, and the record had long stopped playing. Nina had no idea what time it was. She contemplated sleeping there, wondering if she was brave enough to do so, when she heard a loud thump that made her jump. The noise had come from beneath her, from the store, she was sure of it. Another noise came, faint, through the warped floorboards, the sound of something being knocked over.

Was someone really breaking in, already? The lack of respect infuriated her. Nina tip-toed to the front closet. Her father's bat was no longer there, but a golf club was, and she grabbed it, twisting its handle in her hands. Anger coursed through her as she descended the back steps. Maybe she could salvage some of this day after all, take out her aggression on some punk kid's ass in her father's name.

4.

When Nina reached the first-floor landing, she could see the back door had been broken again, the lock she had just replaced lying smashed on the ground. The store was pitch black. She moved slowly, letting her eyes adjust to the darkness. ManDown, his hoodie over his head, a black ski-mask beneath it, stood behind the counter, rifling through paperwork. Nina pulled out her phone, turning on her flashlight, shining it in his eyes.

"If you're looking for money, you picked the wrong store."

ManDown froze, his eyes glowing orange behind the mask. "You need to turn around, Nina, and walk away."

"How the hell do you know my name?"

"You need to leave. While you still can."

"It's you, isn't it? You're ManDown?"

ManDown's eyes burned brighter, and he stepped away from the counter, lurching towards her, as if struggling to control his own body.

Nina fumbled her phone back into her pocket, raising the golf club over her head. "Don't come any closer!"

ManDown stopped, his arms at his sides. Ropes slipped out from the sleeves of his sweatshirt. As they hit the floor, the ropes continued to move on their own, slithering towards Nina, snakes ready to strike.

Nina stepped back, whaling on the ropes with the golf club. They anticipated her movements, as if they were alive, evading her blows. ManDown lunged at her, floating across the floor as he did so, gripping the club mid-swing and hitting her in the chest with his other palm, shoving her to the floor. As he stood over her, the ropes slithered around her, moving up her legs, tightening, a boa-constrictor enveloping its prey. Nina yanked at the ropes, but they were too powerful. "Get them off me!"

ManDown knelt down, his hands gripping her neck. He leaned in close, "Where are the rest?"

"What...are...you talking about?" Nina managed to choke out.

"Where are they?"

ManDown's face was an inch from her own, and Nina could see the fire burning in his eyes, as if real flames licked the backs of his eyeballs. She tried to squirm away, but he held on tight. She managed to slam one knee into his side, a direct hit to his ribs, but he didn't even flinch, only tightening his grip on her throat. Darkness began to cloud her vision, growing with each beat of her heart, pounding in her temples. The ropes moved further up her body, twisting tighter and tighter around her chest.

As Nina lost consciousness, her subconscious began to overflow with unfamiliar images. A crumbling farmhouse, surrounded by a thick pine forest, with dark clouds swirling overhead. A man standing in a window of the house, extremely tall and sickly thin. He wore a wide-brimmed hat, pulled low on his forehead. Three young girls, their backs to her, were playing in the dirt, burning ants with a pair of antique glasses. One by one, the girls turned around, a set of triplets, ten years old, their eyes large black orbs. They smiled at Nina, and their mouths filled with blood.

Out of the shadows, black-gloved hands appeared above ManDown's head, a heavy crucifix chain held taut between them. Killian wrapped the chain around ManDown's neck and wrenched him back, hard. ManDown squealed, letting go of Nina, clawing at the chain. His skin melted beneath it, chunks of flesh oozing through the chain-links. The ropes recoiled from Nina, back up ManDown's sleeves. She could see them circling his body, moving around his chest beneath his shirt.

ManDown spun himself around, grabbing Killian by his lapels. ManDown forced himself to his feet and flung Killian away effortlessly. Killian crashed into a stack of records. ManDown dug the chain out of his neck, tossing it on the floor, hunks of his flesh still dripping from the cross. He fled for the door, then stopped, doubling back to grab a ledger off the counter on the way out.

Killian groaned, rubbing his neck. He crawled to Nina, who was still on the floor, unable to catch her breath.

"Are you okay?" Killian asked.

Nina could only laugh at that, a hoarse, pained chuckle through gasping breaths.

"What do you think?"

Side B: Track 3: An Uneasy Alliance, a Bucket of Blood (4:17)

1.

Killian studied the damage in Reggie's record lounge with a flashlight. Nina stood at the doorway, wary of stepping foot inside the room again. She rubbed the bruises on her neck, wincing in pain. Killian focused his beam on the shattered glass case on the shelf.

"What are you looking for?" Nina asked, her voice still scratchy.

"Not sure, to be honest."

"So, you really think this was all over a record?"

"Three records. Three very rare, and very dangerous records."

"My dad only had one."

"You sure?"

"Pretty sure. What are they?"

"You don't know?"

"No, my dad never let me in here."

"Smart man."

"Attempting to sneak a peek inside this sanctuary was the only time my dad ever laid a hand on me."

"He was trying to protect you."

"From what?" Nina asked.

"You sure he only had the one?"

"I only saw one, I'm pretty sure, when I was a kid. And that's why he came back tonight, right? He asked me where the others were."

Killian sighed. "Your father had a whole set at one point. Wouldn't part with it for any price. Not to me at least."

"You knew my dad?"

"A little. He helped me track down some of the other copies over the years."

"What are they?"

"Do you feel it? The darkness in here? The weight in the air?" Killian rubbed his scar; it came away bloody.

"Are you okay?"

"Have you had any strange dreams lately?"

"Dreams? No."

"I need to find the man who did this."

"I know who did this."

Killian locked eyes with Nina, surprised. "You should have led with that."

2.

Killian and Nina stood on the street in front of the store. Killian studied the crows, still circling in the dark, still fighting with each other. Two of them were dead on the sidewalk, bleeding from cracked beaks.

"How long has this been going on?" Killian asked.

"I just noticed it today."

Killian squatted down, examining the sidewalk.

"What are you looking for?" Nina asked.

"Insects."

Nina stepped back, lifting a shoe. "What? Why?"

Killian stood, grunting in pain, his knees cracking. "What is it you wanted to show me?"

Nina led him across the street to the mural. A small group of onlookers still milled about, grabbing selfies in front of it.

"I know who killed my father, but I don't know who he is," Nina said as they made their way through the small crowd.

"I don't understand."

"Have you ever heard of J. Dilla, MF DOOM, Banksy?"

"What are those?"

"Oh boy..." Nina pointed at the mural before them. "This was made by ManDown, a hip-hop legend, one of the greatest producers of all time, in my opinion. He's also a renowned street artist, who throws ups tags like this in the cities where he's digging for records."

"What's his real name?"

"That's just it. No one knows. It's part of his mystique. He's a total recluse. He's never performed live, never shown his face in public. A lot of people think he's from here, some of his earliest shit was with Detroit MCs, but no one's been able to prove it."

"And you think he killed your father?"

"I mean, he hasn't released any music in like two years, he's been completely M.I.A., and then this mural shows up, across the street from my dad's store, literally the night he's murdered inside of it? And apparently for an ultra-rare record?"

Killian motioned towards the mural. "You're sure this is him, not a copycat?"

"I am. His style would be very difficult to mimic." Nina stepped closer, pointing to a corner of the piece. "The multiple layering here, the fades, this dust effect over here, the double shadows on the edges. It's legit."

Killian stared at her, impressed.

"I went through a bit of a graffiti phase," Nina admitted.

"Do you think your father knew him?"

"Someone would come in every once in a while and spend a lot of cash on records. And never when I was working. And I mean *a lot* of money. Enough to cover a couple months' rent sometimes. I figured it had to be someone famous, a rapper or something, but if I asked my dad about it, he would clam up."

Killian studied the mural again, deep in thought. He turned to Nina, as if he suddenly had a great epiphany. "Are you hungry?"

3.

Nina's diner was busy, even after midnight. The booths surrounding Nina and Killian were filled with the usual spectrum of regulars, drunk college students, two police officers, a middle-aged couple sharing a chocolate malt. A homeless man sat at the counter, sipping on a cup of coffee, taking a brief respite from the abnormally cool night.

Diane brought them a set of menus and two coffees. "You're out late tonight, Nina."

"Yeah, working on the store. Thanks again for coming to the funeral."

"You know I wouldn't have missed it for the world."

"It meant a lot."

Diane smiled, a tear in her eye. She knocked her knuckles on the Formica table. "This will always be your father's booth, as far as I'm concerned. I'll be back in a few to take your order." She nodded at Killian, "Father," and headed to the kitchen.

Killian was momentarily confused. "Oh, shit." He yanked the clerical collar out of his shirt, quickly undoing his top button.

Nina burst out laughing. "So, you're not really a priest?"

"Oh no, I am, I just try not to advertise it."

"Only when you're, say, breaking and entering into a record shop?"

"It's a good thing I did, isn't it? But yes, this collar has come in handy with the police on more than one occasion." He tossed it on the seat next to him.

"Man, I wish I had one of those."

"I could probably find you a habit, if you want."

"I might burst into flames if I put one of those on. No offense."

"None taken. I wonder if that will happen to me every time I put that damn thing around my neck."

Nina studied him. "You're not at all what I picture when I think of a priest."

Killian held up his mug of coffee in a mock cheers. "Thank you. That's the nicest thing someone's said to me in a long time."

Diane came back. "What're we having?"

Killian picked up his menu, perusing it quickly. "What's good?"

"I'll just have coffee, thanks."

"You sure? I'm buying," Killian said.

Nina thought about it, "Okay, then I'll have the half-stack, two eggs over-easy, hashbrowns extra crispy, a side of bacon, extra, extra crispy, and a large OJ."

Killian handed his menu to the waitress. "Make that two of those."

Killian and Nina ate their food in silence, enjoying the piping hot towers of grease. Killian poked an egg yolk with his bacon. "What did he take with him tonight? ManDown. Off the counter."

Nina took a long drink of her orange juice. "My dad's ledger."

"If your father sold the other two records, would that have been in there?"

"Absolutely. My dad was very old-school, every transaction written by hand."

"It's imperative that he doesn't find those other records."

"What are they?"

"Very dangerous."

"I have to say, I'm getting a little tired of that answer."

"It's for your own good. Trust me."

"How much are we talking, for the records he sold?" Nina asked.

"He could name his price."

"Henry Watts."

"Who's that?"

"That's who would have bought them, no question. My dad's oldest friend. They were in a couple bands together, back in the day. He's been collecting vinyl even longer than my dad, and he has bottomless pockets."

"Where is he?"

"Philly."

"Then that's where I'm headed."

"When are we leaving?"

Killian set down his fork. "It's too dangerous. Trust me, you don't want to be involved in this."

"I'm already involved. He murdered my father. I'm coming with you."

"I can't let..."

"And no offense, Father, but you're a little out of your depth here. You need my help, and you know it." Nina stared at him, intense, unblinking. "I'm the only reason you have any leads at all, remember?"

Killian threw up his hands, a surrender. "Alright, alright! Let's get the bill."

On their way out the door, Killian stopped, exchanging a few words with the homeless man at the counter, his hand resting on his shoulder. He gave him his leftovers in a box, with a ten-dollar bill on top of it.

The man nodded his thanks and Killian caught up to Nina, "Okay, let's go." He held the door for her. Nina couldn't help but smile as they headed out into the cold night together.

4.

ManDown sat on the ground in his backyard, his back against the house. Tears welled in his eyes. "Please. Don't make me do this. I don't think I can do this," ManDown muttered to himself.

His body went stiff, rigid. The ropes moved again, slithering beneath his shirt, tightening around his chest. ManDown grimaced in pain, biting his lower lip. His eyes flickered with flames, growing brighter. ManDown pulled out his cellphone and made a call.

***

ManDown sat before the monitors in his bunker. The record played on a turntable at full blast, while digital recordings of it played from his laptop, the sounds mixing and echoing with each other. ManDown adjusted the levels, four different versions playing, overlapping, a blistering wall of horrific sound, now with an808 drum beat pulsing through it.

Behind him, his drug dealer, the guy who'd sold him weed for over ten years, hung by his feet from a pipe in the ceiling. A chunk of bloody rope bound his feet, digging into his ankles. His throat was slit open, a butcher's knife lying on the floor beneath him next to a bucket. The bucket caught the blood spilling from his gullet. The bucket was overflowing, blood spreading across the concrete floor.

ManDown grabbed the pail and slid it towards himself. He pushed up a sleeve and reached beneath the crimson surface. He pulled out Reggie's ledger. ManDown leafed through its blood-soaked pages, until he found a single sheet that was still dry, bright white, untouched by the plasma. He watched as drops of blood slowly soaked through the page. The drops moved on their own, connecting with one another, forming a circle around a single name, '*Henry Watts.*'

ManDown grimaced again. He pulled up his shirt, his chest was chaffed, bleeding, raw. The ropes swirled around his body, moving inside him, beneath his flesh: in through a small wound under his ribcage, reemerging bloody from another wound beneath his armpit, tightening further. He shivered, closing his eyes, a concoction of revulsion and ecstasy pulsing through his body. The music grew louder, the whispering static stretching his speakers to their breaking point. When he opened his eyes again, they burned with an all-consuming fire.

Side B: Interlude 2: We've Made a Grave Mistake (2:24)

In early 1944, Father Clint Bennett, newly appointed as Chancellor of Saint John's Catholic University, made an urgent request to the Vatican. After a long back and forth up and down the chain of command, Father Bennett was granted an emergency meeting with Cardinal Salvatore, which occurred on Thursday, January 27th, at approximately 11:00 AM. As was standard practice, Salvatore's secretary of thirty years took notes for the Vatican archives.

The following is a portion of the transcript from said meeting. Names have been redacted to preserve the privacy of the victims and their families.

SALVATORE: Was everyone affected?

BENNETT: No. There were thirty students in my class, and nine of them felt side-effects.

SALVATORE: Does that include XXXXXXXX?

BENNETT: It does.

SALVATORE: What did the other eight experience?

BENNETT: It ran the gamut. A few just had headaches, nausea, some vomited. Others experienced heightened emotions, anxiety, and ill tempers. One student, XXXXXXXX, had suicidal thoughts, but was still able to distinguish reality. He asked for help before acting on the impulses, thankfully.

SALVATORE: Were his parents notified?

BENNETT: No sir. And that was his choice, by the way.

SALVATORE: Good. How about you?

BENNETT: Me?

SALVATORE: Any symptoms?

BENNETT: Some mild nausea, and horrible nightmares, images I dare not even speak aloud.

SALVATORE: And you believe the Martel recordings caused XXXXXXXX to do what he did?

BENNETT: I do, sir. He became obsessed with them, checking them out of the library, studying them at night in his dormitory.

SALVATORE: I realize this is a delicate subject, and I don't mean to sound insensitive, but do you feel the police suspect any connection between XXXXXXXX's actions and Saint John's, or the church for that matter?

BENNETT: No sir, and I was there.

SALVATORE: You were there?

BENNETT: As soon as I heard the news, I took the train there, to XXXXX. I didn't know he was already dead. I was still hoping I could help him in some way.

SALVATORE: It's hard to believe, isn't it? One of ours, going home for Christmas, killing their own mother, and then hanging themself?

BENNETT: It's a scene I'll never forget, Your Eminence.

SALVATORE: I don't doubt it. So, what do you propose?

BENNETT: We need to pull the records from the curriculum, immediately.

SALVATORE: How many seminaries received them?

BENNETT: That's partly why I'm here. I don't know how many copies were produced.

SALVATORE: What a mess, a mess I feel responsible for.

BENNETT: You, why?

SALVATORE: I pushed for new tools, you know, a new, more modern curriculum to help us fight the ever-changing face of evil in our world.

BENNETT: No one could have known, Your Eminence. No one could have imagined the absolute depravity pressed into those records. There's something in them, a darkness that is beyond our comprehension, I fear.

SALVATORE: How do you mean?

BENNETT: I don't think they're normal entities. Not that normal is the right word for any demonic force loose in our world. But they seem more powerful than the others. Studying them, I believe they might be from a hierarchy we haven't encountered yet.

SALVATORE: Well, Father Bennett, I appreciate your swift action regarding this matter, as well as your discretion. We will discuss this internally and get back to you shortly with a plan of action.

BENNETT: Thank you, Your Eminence, and thank you again for seeing me on such short notice. I am here to help in any way that I can.

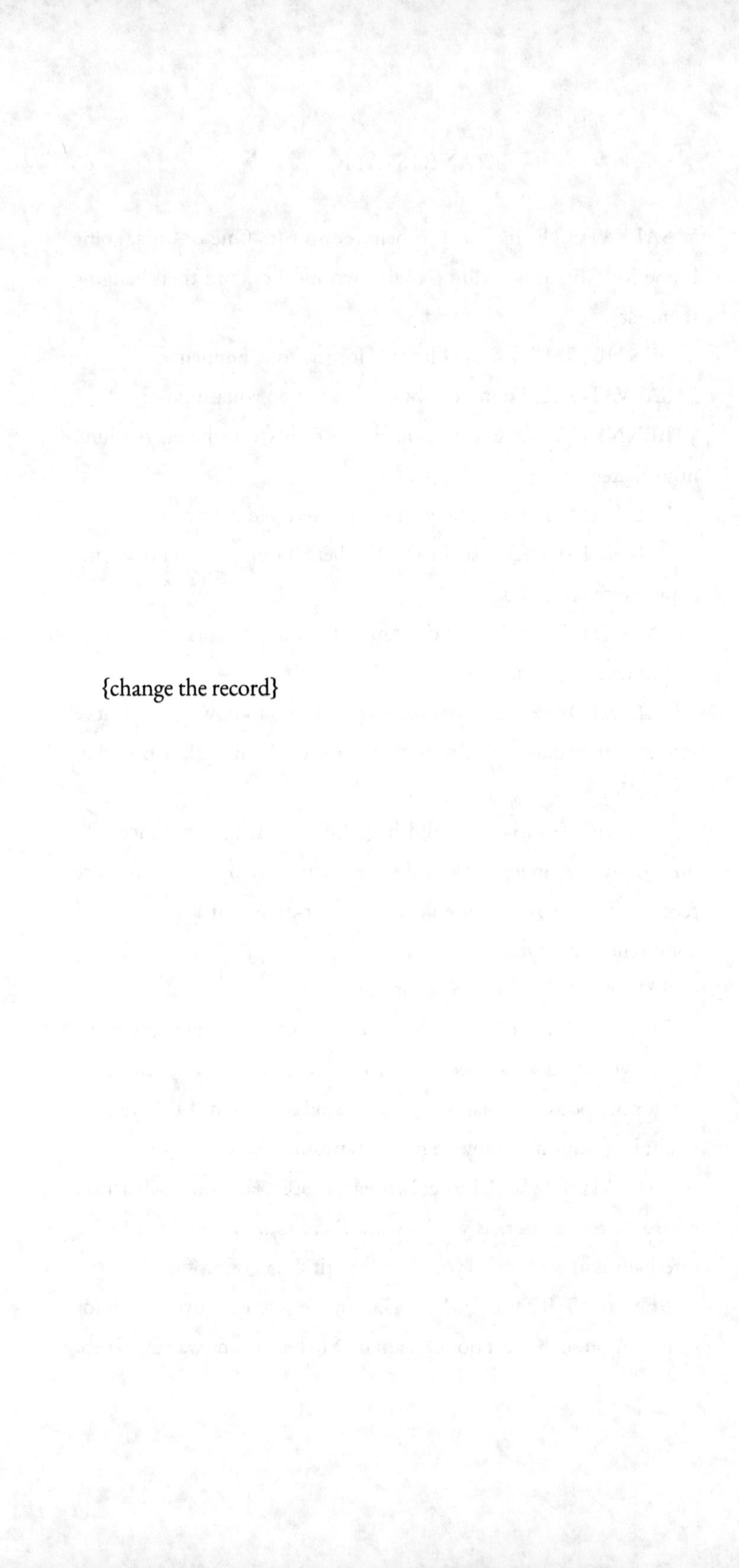

{change the record}

Side C: Track 1: When One Door Opens... (3:58)

1.

Killian drove his thirty-year-old sedan down Highway 76, heading east towards the rising sun. He was enjoying the open road, pushing the aging engine to its limit. There was little traffic, a rarity on the east coast. Nina sat in the passenger seat, sipping on gas-station coffee.

"All that money you guys got, and the Vatican couldn't spring for a flight? No first-class? Nothing?"

"The Vatican? They like to pretend I don't exist."

"Why's that?"

"I tend to make trouble."

"Is that why you're a librarian?"

"Not exactly."

"That's gotta be a demotion for a priest, right?"

"No."

"Like a cop stuck on desk duty?"

"I served as a priest, just after seminary. It didn't last long."

"What happened?"

"It was a small parish in upstate New York. I immediately butted heads with them."

"Why?"

"They were elderly, ultra-conservative. It was just never going to work. Plus, I beat up a Cardinal on the front steps of the church."

Nina's eyes went wide. "How'd that happen?"

"He was a pompous, arrogant man, completely full of himself."

"That's it?"

"And he was rumored to be a long-time abuser of children."

Nina shook her head, "Good for you."

"After that, I found myself back at St. John's."

"And what do you do now, exactly, other than file books?"

"I protect the church's secrets. Sacred texts, artifacts, anything that might pose a threat."

"A threat to who? The public, or the church's pocketbooks?"

Killian didn't respond, focusing on the road in front of him.

"See, that's my problem with you guys," Nina continued.

"Meaning?"

"Organized religion in general. You shouldn't be allowed to have any secrets."

"Okay, shoot. What do you want to know?" Killian switched lanes, passing a semi-truck.

"What are these records?"

Killian sighed; he had put it off as long as he could. "An exorcism."

Nina stared at him, "Okay."

"For a short period of time, the church recorded them, with the idea that they could be used to help teach young priests how to perform them."

"Well, that seems like a terrible idea."

"In retrospect, yes. Especially in this case. The effect of this specific set on some students was extreme, to say the least."

"Like what?"

"I won't go into specifics, but in one case, the results were fatal."

"Just from listening? How is that even possible?"

"The church doesn't know. It only happened with this set."

"What do you think?"

"I think it happened because this particular exorcism dealt with multiple, very powerful, very unusual forces, and it wasn't successful. I think pieces of the demons, their power, something, was trapped in these records. They seem to cause a sort of semi-possession, a tethering of some kind. And then we went and made copies of them."

"Demons?" Nina tried to laugh it off.

"You saw it with your own eyes, what they can do to a person. Do you have a sane explanation for anything you've experienced in the last week?"

"So, it's like a possession micro-dose. How have I not heard about this?"

"The program was shut down. I've been tracking down these records for 40 years now, destroying every one I can find."

"Don't you think this is something the public should be warned about?"

"The church's position, and mine as well, is that admitting to their existence would only make them more valuable, even more sought after."

"How many copies are out there?"

"That's the problem. I'm not sure. Copies were produced and distributed to seminaries all over the world. I think I've found most of them, but I can't be certain."

Killian took an off ramp, pulling into a gas station. "The internet has helped me immensely in some respects, and at the same time it's made my job much more difficult. I fear that more people know about these records now than ever before." Killian parked at a pump. "Need to use the restroom?"

"Can the Vatican at least spring for some road snacks?" Nina asked.

When Killian pulled back onto the highway, he and Nina both sipped from giant fountain sodas, a bag of sour cream and onion chips and a large package of gummy worms between them.

"Ooh, you still have a tape deck!" Nina said, rooting around in her backpack.

"You have tapes? Tapes are still a thing?"

Nina pulled a cassette from her bag. "Oh yeah. You can learn something while you drive." She popped it in the deck. Dark, instrumental hip-hop beats filled the car, eerie and menacing.

"What is this?"

"This is Symphony of Screams, Volume One. The original version, before ManDown cleaned it up for the re-release. A mistake if you ask me. This version is much better."

Nina watched Killian listen to the unusual sounds, confusion growing on his face, his forehead wrinkling. She tried not to laugh. He reached forward and turned up the volume.

"Wow, I thought this would be a hard pass. I thought for sure you were shutting it off."

Killian listened to the beat, tilting his ear towards the speaker in his door. "Is that Faure's Requiem I'm hearing?"

"Ha! I bet it is. Nice catch. He sampled a lot of classical back then, a lot of old choral pieces."

"Interesting."

"You like it?"

"I didn't say that."

Nina turned off the tape. "I won't subject you to anymore. Can't say I feel like listening to the man that killed my father either."

Killian checked the odometer, "Can you type the address in your phone, make sure there's no construction or anything up ahead?"

"No can do."

Killian glanced at her, "What do you mean? Why not?"

"I don't have a smartphone; I don't even have internet."

"You're kidding."

"I'm not. My phone's older than yours."

"Wow. If I'm the technologically savvy one on our team, we're in some real trouble."

2.

The sun was setting as they rode into the city of Philadelphia, a fiery globe disappearing behind them. Killian parked on a long, winding street on the outskirts of the city across from a massive Victorian home. It had once been an impressive piece of architecture, but now its paint was peeling, its roof missing shingles, its shutters lying broken in tall grass.

Killian studied the house, the less-than-perfect neighborhood. "I thought you said this guy was wealthy?"

"Oh, he is, believe me. Inherited a small fortune from his grandmother. He only spends it on one thing though."

Nina and Killian stood on the front steps. A security camera buzzed above them. A dozen 'No Solicitors' signs were taped to the front door. A 'BEWARE OF DOG' sign was staked into the lawn near the walkway.

"You sure you're ready for this?" Nina asked.

"Ready for what? What do you mean?"

"Just you wait."

Nina rang the doorbell. They waited, no one answered.

"Maybe he's not home?" Killian asked.

"He's home, no question." Nina rang the bell again, buzzing it several times in a row.

A scratchy voice came from the intercom above the doorbell. "Whatever you're selling, I'm not buying! Can't you read a goddamn sign?"

Nina leaned into the intercom. "How about a mint, sealed copy of Yesterday and Today, the butcher cover?"

There was a long pause, only feedback. "Nina? Is that really you?"

3.

Henry Watt's house was like nothing Killian had ever seen. There were well over a hundred thousand records packed inside it. Every wall was floor to ceiling shelving, and every shelf was sagging under the weight of hundreds of pounds of vinyl. In addition to the walls, every other surface was covered, every table, counter, ottoman, chair, even the kitchen counters. An open cabinet door revealed even more records where there should have been dishes.

The floor itself was littered with countless piles several feet high. Killian could see that the hallway leading to the back of the house was lined with records as well, on each wall, leaving only a few feet between them for walking. Killian wasn't normally claustrophobic, but the whole place gave him anxiety. He stared at the ceiling above them with trepidation, wondering how much additional weight was stuffed into the second floor, and how much longer the old bones of the house could bear it.

Henry led them through the intricate labyrinth to his living room couch. He cleared a stack of records from the cushions, opening a small space for Killian to sit. As he sunk into the worn cushion, the stacks of records on each side tilted in, resting against his shoulders.

Henry was skin and bones, all nervous energy. He went to the kitchen to grab coffees. Nina immediately sat cross-legged on the floor, scouring a pile of old jazz records. Killian's jaw hung half-open, trying to process his surroundings.

Henry came back carrying three mugs. "You like that?" Henry asked Nina.

"Holy shit, Henry. There's some amazing stuff in here."

"Right? An old drummer I knew passed away. Played all over this city for decades. His widow reached out to me."

Nina held up records, still sealed. "Some of these haven't even been opened!"

"He owned at least three copies of everything. I've barely scratched the surface of his collection."

Henry handed them each a mug of coffee. He cleared more records off a wooden chair and sat down. He took in the shock on Killian's face. "I take it you're not a collector?"

"I own a bed, a chair, and maybe a dozen books?"

Nina and Henry stared at him like he was an alien.

"And you bring this man into my home?" Henry said with a grin.

"He's alright. I think," Nina replied.

Henry turned to Nina, "Hey, I'm really sorry about your dad, and I'm truly sorry I didn't make it to the funeral."

"Thank you, and no worries at all. I know you don't get out much."

"Yeah, I think I heard something about a pandemic out there? How'd that go?"

"Fuck you."

"I knew being agoraphobic would pay off one day! Seriously though, what brings you all the way here?"

Killian leaned forward. "The Martel records."

Henry slumped in his chair. "Is that what happened to Reggie? Over those damn records? I knew it. I knew it was only a matter of time. I wish your old man had never stumbled upon those cursed things."

"Where did he find them?" Nina asked.

"Just dumb luck. An old church closed out in the burbs, had a big yard sale. He found them in a crate of old choral records. Paid two bucks for them, I think."

Killian was still anxious, not just from his surroundings, but from the fact that he had no idea where ManDown was, and if he was on his way there. He eyed the doors, windows, figuring out an exit plan if one was needed. He couldn't take it any longer. "So, where are the records? The other two?"

Henry stood up, scanning his walls. "Let's see." He ran his fingers along a shelf, a filing system only he could understand. "Here she is." He pulled out a record in a blank sleeve, the inner circle visible, the red label, the number two stenciled on the edge.

Nina jumped up, snatching it from his hands. "Damn, Henry! There's not even a plastic sleeve on this thing!"

"Hiding in plain sight, right?"

Killian snatched the record from Nina, setting it gently on the coffee table. "You have to be careful with that."

"Even touching it?" Nina asked.

"You never know how it can affect you. Where's the other one?"

Henry gave them a sheepish grin. "About that…"

"What did you do, Henry?" Nina asked.

"I sold it."

"What? When?"

"Couple years back."

"To whom?" Killian asked.

Henry seemed embarrassed to answer. He finally responded, a half-whisper. "Ray Wise."

"Ray Wise? No fucking way." Nina groaned.

"Who's that?" Killian asked.

"You sold it to the *Pharma Bro*?" Nina was incensed.

"This was before all that came out."

Nina turned to Killian. "He's a Wall Street billionaire piece of shit. Buys patents on drugs, raises the prices to astronomical levels. The dude is shameless. A legendary collector though. If it's rare and expensive, he wants it." Nina shook her head at Henry, scolding him. "I thought you were rich, man?"

"Not that rich! He made me an offer way too good to pass up. Like, I have health insurance now, kind-of-money!"

"Where does he live?" Killian asked.

"New York," Nina replied.

"Any chance his name would have been in your dad's ledger? He ever do business with him?"

"No, my dad hated him, refused to sell him anything."

"Reggie was always a better man than I," Henry said.

"So, on to New York?" Nina asked.

"If ManDown finds Henry in that ledger, he's going to want more than just this record. You're the only link to the third one, Henry," Killian said.

"Well shit. That's not very reassuring."

"Can't we just destroy this one right now? Maybe, he could feel it? Maybe he wouldn't bother showing up?" Nina asked Killian.

"I couldn't risk it, doing it here, it's too powerful. Sometimes they don't want to be destroyed."

"What does that mean?"

"I think we're staying the night, Henry. Just to be safe."

4.

The sun had fully set, and Killian made his way through Henry's house, sprinkling holy water from a small flask he carried in his jacket pocket on the windowsills and door frames. On the front and back doors, he hung crucifixes from the doorknobs. He doubted it would do much good, but it made him feel a little bit safer at least. He double-checked Henry's security system. The keypad confirmed it was set for the night.

Nina and Henry sat on the couch, sipping tea. Nina stared at the record. "You ever listen to it?"

"Only once, and I couldn't even get through the whole thing."

"What happened?"

"Nothing, at first. Then I had the worst nightmares I've ever had in my life. Those poor girls. The visions lasted for over a month."

"What girls?"

Henry stared at her. "You don't know, the triplets?"

Nina motioned towards Killian, his back to them. "He won't tell me shit."

"I don't know much. I was scared to do too much research, to be honest. All I know is that it was three young sisters, triplets, who were possessed. That's who's recorded on this set."

"Jesus. Did my dad listen to them?"

"Once, at least. You don't believe it, you know? It's hard not to find out for yourself."

"Do you know how he reacted?"

"Better than most, just a headache. At least that's what he told me." Henry made sure Killian was still out of earshot. He leaned in, whispering, "You trust this guy, Nina?"

"Not sure yet, but he did save my life."

"And this dude, ManDown? He really thinks he's coming here for this record?"

"He killed my father for his."

Killian joined them, slumping into a ratty old recliner. He let out a sigh as he settled in, his knees welcoming the rest.

"You feel better?" Nina asked him.

"Not really."

"I have a state-of-the-art security system. He's not getting in here," Henry said.

"I hope you're right."

"So, what do we do now?" Nina asked.

"We wait," Killian replied.

Nina thought about what Henry said: three young girls, triplets. That's who she had seen when ManDown touched her. What did that mean? Was she one of the ones more susceptible to the power of the records? She was tempted to ask Killian but decided to keep it to herself.

5.

Just after midnight, all was quiet in Henry's house. The alarm touchscreen blinked green in the dark living room. Killian dozed in the recliner, and Nina was asleep on the couch. The record sat on the coffee table between them.

Its proximity to Nina altered her dream state, filling her subconscious with disturbing images: flashes of an attic room with a vaulted ceiling, three small beds all in a row, ropes slithering up the walls, three sets of black eyes, filling her mind, infecting her with their menace.

In the back of the house, Henry slept on an old, lumpy twin mattress, a box spring its only bedframe. His floor was littered with dirty clothes, his walls covered with more records, overflowing shelves from the floor to the ceiling. His dreams were similar to Nina's, dreams he hadn't had in many years. His eyes moved back and forth behind their lids as he murmured in his sleep, trying to flee the whispering cackles of the triplets.

In the corner of the room, a doorway appeared, a silent black rectangle solidifying, a cool breeze flowing from it. ManDown stepped through silently. He stood over Henry's sleeping body, the ropes swirling around his chest, his eyes burning. He stood there for a long time, watching Henry fight his nightmares, relishing in his fear.

Nina woke with a start, gasping. Something was crawling on her hand. She looked down and found a large cockroach, several inches long, moving up her arm, tunneling under her sleeve. She jumped to her feet, shaking it off. Killian didn't wake. She grabbed a shoe to kill it, but it had already disappeared into the darkness. Nina shook her head in disgust, "Jesus, Henry, it's time to clean your fucking house."

There was a thud at the end of the hallway. Nina tip-toed towards it. "Henry, you okay?"

A swarm of cockroaches skittered between her feet, their onyx backs shining in the darkness as they raced down the hallway. Nina jumped. "Jesus!" The roaches slipped under Henry's door. The doorway opened slowly, just a crack. A thick rope snaked out, slithering along the floorboards towards Nina, leaving a crimson trail of blood.

Nina bolted back, "Killian!"

Nina made it to the living room as Killian woke up. "What! What's wrong?"

Before Nina could answer, the rope caught up to her. It wrapped around her leg, yanking her to the floor, dragging her down the hallway. Nina screamed; Killian groggily stumbled after her. He froze when he reached the hallway. ManDown was coming towards him, dragging a bloody Henry by the arm. Nina was on the floor between them, the ropes moving up her body, tightening their grip, squeezing the air out of her lungs.

"Where is it?" ManDown's voice was no longer his own. It sounded like several people yelling over each other, just out of sync, echoing in the tight hallway.

Killian pulled a crucifix from his pocket, raising it up in the air. "Let them go!"

ManDown barreled down the hallway towards Killian, still dragging Henry with him. The ropes let go of Nina as he stepped around her, following their master.

"I command you to stop, in the name of the Lord!" Killian screamed.

ManDown grabbed Killian by the neck, lifting him into the air, tossing him aside into a wall. ManDown grabbed the record from the table, the fire in his eyes glowing brighter as soon as he touched it. In the corner of the living room, another doorway appeared, ManDown's bunker visible on the other side. ManDown headed towards it, the record in one hand, Henry's arm in the other.

"Let me go!" Henry screamed.

Nina rushed into the room, gasping for breath. She lunged for Henry. Killian tried to stand up, but couldn't, his bruised knees leaving him in agony.

"Stop him!" Killian yelled.

Nina dove onto the floor, gripping Henry's foot. She slowed them down, but ManDown was too powerful. He kept moving, slowly drawing them towards the doorway.

"Hold on, Henry!" Nina yelled.

"Help me!"

ManDown reached the doorway and crossed the threshold. Henry was partially through it. Nina dug her feet into the floor, holding Henry back. His eyes were wide with terror, his neck muscles bulging as he tried to break free of ManDown's grip.

The doorway disappeared, severing Henry's leg just below the knee. With the rest of him gone, Nina flew back, landing on her ass, still holding his leg, the end of it a blackened, cauterized stump.

"Jesus Christ!" Nina tossed the leg on the floor, bile rising in her throat. Killian slowly crawled to her side and sat back down. He rubbed his knees. His scar was bleeding profusely, seeping down his neck.

"I couldn't stop him, I..." Nina began.

"I've never seen that much power from listening to just one of the records."

"He's not just listening to it."

"What do you mean?"

"He's a producer. He's probably making a beat with it, chopping it up, putting it back together, maybe playing it backwards, changing the pitch. Who knows what he came up with?"

"Then he can never find the third one."

"What would happen if he had all three?"

Killian ignored her question, perhaps afraid of the answer. "If Henry's still alive, it's only a matter of time before he gets him to talk."

"Then we need to get to Ray Wise before he does."

"We need to make a stop first."

Nina stared at Henry's severed leg lying between them. "That's fucked up."

They sat in silence.

"Yes, it is," Killian replied.

Side C: Track 2: A Concrete Grave, a Glass Castle (2:47)

1.

Henry dreamed of the triplets for the second time that night. The girls were dressed in matching white nightgowns, tied down to three small beds with thick ropes, all in a row. Henry was in the room with them, a paralyzed fly on the wall. The triplets' faces were gaunt, strained, pale. They writhed in their beds, the ropes moving with them, clutching them tight, not letting go.

A priest stood over them, shaking holy water on their bodies. They squirmed as it hit their skin. The girls hissed, screaming back at him in an unknown tongue. Blood seeped through their cotton gowns, boils on their bodies forming and popping beneath the coiling ropes. The girls froze, growing silent, their bodies stiff. One by one, they swiveled their heads, fixing their collective gaze on Henry.

Henry tried to turn away, to run, but he was frozen in place. Their eyes grew black, as if oil sprung forth from deep inside their skulls, pooling behind their sockets. Their mouths opened, slowly, in unison, their jaws cracking loudly, the flesh of their cheeks tearing, their chins touching their chests.

Low, guttural moans rose from deep within their torsos, reverberating around the small room. Crows exploded from their mouths, ripping their way out of split lips. The crows attacked Henry, swirling around him, pecking at his chest, his eyes.

Henry woke up screaming and found himself in a much worse place. He was tied to a chair in ManDown's bunker, a single bare bulb burning above him. It took a few seconds for the pain pulsating up from his leg to reach his brain. He looked down and saw the charred stump. Beads of blood soaked through the blackened skin, dripping onto the floor. He could smell his own cooked flesh hanging in the air. Henry didn't stop screaming for a long time.

ManDown ignored Henry's cries for help, focusing on his vast array of boards and monitors. Both records now spun on turntables. With the additional record, the triplets' screams were transforming into a complex chorus, teetering on the edge of a symphony. ManDown adjusted the various knobs, levels, cranking the volume higher and higher, drowning out Henry's shrieks.

ManDown added another layer of sound into the mix, and Henry realized it was his own scream, recorded just seconds ago, now echoing back at him. This finally shut Henry up. His body convulsing from the pain, he was reduced to whimpers, praying that he would pass out again. His prayers would go unanswered.

ManDown kept mixing, manipulating the sounds, until the second record began to spin faster and faster. Shadowy tendrils escaped its grooves, testing the air, encircling ManDown, sizing him up. Satisfied, they poured themselves into his body, tunneling into his nose and mouth. ManDown's body trembled, the ropes tightening around him. They stretched around Henry as well, and that was when Henry realized the ropes that held him were also a part of ManDown, running down his legs, snaking across the cement floor and up Henry's chair.

Despite the agony he was in, Henry began to rock the chair back and forth. He scanned the room, seeking a way out, however slim his chances were of an escape. As he craned his neck behind him, he found the drug dealer still hanging from the ceiling. He was beginning to rot, the flesh on his face raw, his torso swelling with gas. Lines of ants moved up and down the rope from the pipe above him, feasting on the open flesh of his ankles. Henry swallowed bile and began to rock faster. Maybe an attempted escape might at least buy him a quick death.

Just as he was about to fall back onto the floor, ManDown whirled around, slamming the chair back down with his foot. As the chair hit the floor, the music abruptly stopped, plunging the bunker into a silence that made Henry's ears ring. ManDown leaned in close, both hands clutching the arms of the chair, his eyes glowing with fire.

"Where's the other one?" ManDown asked.

"What other one?"

"Don't fuck with me. The third record."

"I don't know anything about three records, man. I only had the one." ManDown stared at him, unblinking. Henry continued, pleading, "I swear, I won't say anything. You already have my record. Let me go, please!"

ManDown shoved his hand into Henry's stomach, his fingers effortlessly cutting through the flesh like a white-hot blade. Henry could feel ManDown's arm inside him, moving through his body, bisecting his stomach, tearing through his intestines, his fingers clawing their way up and behind his ribcage. Blood poured from Henry's nose and mouth. ManDown flexed his hand inside of Henry, and his mouth began to move, opening and closing, a cadaverous ventriloquist dummy.

Henry spoke his final words. "Ray...Wise."

ManDown ripped his arm out of Henry's chest, and he slumped in the chair, a ragdoll. ManDown shook the excess gore from his arm onto the floor. The flames in his eyes grew brighter, the lights flickered, and the bulb above him exploded, showering him in shards of glass.

Outside, the crows swirled above the bunker, their cackles a siren in the night as they tore each other apart, their black feathers floating gently towards the grass below.

2.

Killian was happy to be back on his home turf, even if it was only for a brief visit. He and Nina walked the commons of Saint John's University, heading towards the archives. Above the building, hundreds of crows flew in aggressive circles that steadily grew wider.

"That's not a good sign, I take it?" Nina asked.

Killian pointed to a line of ants on the ground. "All scavengers it seems, are drawn to true darkness, to the rot of pure evil."

"You should be a poet."

Killian unlocked the library door and led Nina inside. She marveled at the towers of books surrounding them as they made their way through the dark space.

"And you said you weren't a collector."

"I inherited all of this. Believe me, I don't want it." He pulled the bookcase out, revealing the hidden archives door.

Nina was impressed. "Now we're talking! I've been waiting for the super-secret church conspiracy shit."

Nina was even more awestruck by what lay behind the door. She ran her hands along the shelves, taking it all in. She leaned down, peering into glass cases containing ancient scrolls, stone sculptures, jeweled talismans. "I'm probably the first person who isn't an old white dude to see all this, huh?"

Killian thought about that, admitting, "Yes, that's probably correct."

Nina shook her head. "How long has all this been here?"

"Most of it was smuggled out of Europe during World War II. The church had been fearful of certain secrets falling into the wrong hands. Rather than having everything in one place, they made the decision to scatter their secrets across the world."

Nina started to open a glass case that housed a large chunk of jade, inscribed with symbols she didn't recognize. Killian quickly shut it. "You don't want to mess with that."

"Why not?"

"Just trust me. That's not why we're here."

Killian went to the crates on the wall, and Nina joined him, watching the ants swarm the bleeding records.

"You saved copies?"

"Just one set, the original acetates."

"Why?"

"I didn't like the idea of the only copies left being out in the wild somewhere, possibly in the wrong hands. I hoped it might help us, someday, having our own."

Nina studied the crate. "So, these were actually, physically in the room, with those poor girls?"

"That's right, recording their terror live, as it happened."

Nina reached forward, ready to touch them. Killian gripped her arm, gently lowering it. "Which means they were also in the same room as something else, Nina, something truly evil and extremely powerful."

Nina shook her head. Her mind had drifted there for a second. She had been back at the farmhouse, staring up at three shadows in an upstairs window looking down upon her. She took a step back.

"They sneak up on you, don't they?" Killian said.

"They do."

"We'll be out of here in a minute. I just need to grab a few things."

Killian searched the shelves, finding what he needed. He piled several antique crucifixes on a small table, along with a flask and a small, leather-bound book. He handed Nina a larger iron crucifix, its metal blackened, chipped.

"What am I supposed to do with this?"

Killian took it back and pulled it apart, revealing an ivory dagger hidden beneath a sheath.

"Okay, that's pretty badass," Nina said.

Killian poured holy water from the flask onto the blade and handed it back to her, "I honestly don't know what, if anything, will work at this point, but it can't hurt."

"What is this made of?"

"The blade? It's carved from bone."

"Human?"

"You don't want to know."

"Okay." Nina scrunched her face and carefully slid the blade back into place. "How old is it?"

"A few thousand years, give or take. It's supposedly a very powerful weapon."

"Cool, and totally, totally normal." Nina tucked the crucifix into a jacket pocket, still taking in everything on the shelves. "All of this knowledge, all of this power, just sitting here, gathering dust."

"You've seen what happens when it gets out."

"So, do you think this was the demons' plan, just bide their time until someone decoded the recordings or whatever it is that ManDown's done?"

"I think they just became trapped. I don't think they had the ability to predict the future, the advancements in technology that could one day set them free. Truthfully, I think it's just bad luck."

"It's bad luck for us, that's for sure."

3.

Nina and Killian made their way to Killian's apartment building, a converted dormitory on the edge of campus. The same dorm he lived in while in seminary. In the cramped lobby, its yellow carpet worn down by years of foot traffic, its green walls cracked and peeling, four elderly men sat around a card table, working on a puzzle of an Italian coastline. They stopped what they were doing, staring at Nina as they entered the elevator.

As the doors closed, Killian chuckled. "You're really going to set off the busy bodies in here."

"This is where you live?"

"Is it that bad?"

"I didn't mean it like that! You just seem way too young for a place like this. What is it?"

"It's where priests go to die."

Nina bit her tongue. The lurching elevator smelled of antiseptic and broccoli, with just a hint of urine, much like her grandmother's nursing home, a place Nina feared for much of her childhood.

Killian's apartment was at the end of a long dark hallway on the third floor. His single window overlooked the campus commons below. Nina sat in an old, worn recliner while Killian washed up in the small half-bathroom attached to his room. The former dorm room had been renovated into a studio apartment, even smaller than her own. Aside from the chair she sat in, there was a twin bed, a rickety nightstand, and a short row of books on a granite windowsill. On the wall, next to a corner kitchenette, was a single framed photograph of his parents, the only personal item of any kind on display. In one corner of the ceiling, a water stain was slowly making its way towards the center of the room, like a rain cloud encroaching the horizon.

It was, in a word, depressing. Nina felt bad for thinking it, for judging a man she barely knew, but she couldn't imagine anyone living a happy, fulfilling life in this solitary place. She made a pact with herself, right then and there, that she wouldn't end up like this, alone in her tiny apartment, fifty years from now, with only her records to keep her company.

"You don't seem too impressed." Killian was standing next to her, buttoning up a fresh shirt.

"No, it's nice. You should see my place."

"It's not as bad as it looks. You should see it on poker night."

"Poker night?"

"Give these old-timers enough whiskey, and you can really take them to the cleaners."

"I would love to see that."

"You have an open invitation."

"I'm holding you to that. Once this is over, I am taking all your money!"

4.

Ray Wise, a tall, scrawny weasel of a man, paced back and forth in his living room, his silk bathrobe half-open. He could only stop long enough to snort a line of cocaine from a glass coffee table, chasing it down with a twenty-dollar swig of whisky, before continuing his manic figure-eight. His penthouse was floor-to-ceiling windows, all glass and steel, a twenty-million-dollar view of Central Park below. He was surrounded by garish furniture, elaborate wall hangings, and statues of naked women, his taste falling somewhere between Scarface and a Frat-house run by Caligula.

Ray's personal bodyguard, Brick, sat at the end of a long-dining room table, reading a magazine. The man embodied his name, a rectangular, six-foot wall of chiseled muscle. He eyed his boss with consternation. "Sir, with all due respect, maybe it's time to call it a night?"

Ray wheeled around, grabbing a Detroit newspaper from the table. He held up the obituary page, Reggie's face in the corner, the paper crinkling in his hands. "You think this is a good time to get some beauty sleep?" Ray threw down the newspaper and stormed out of the room. Brick rolled his eyes, reluctantly following him.

Ray stood in his library, which he had transformed into a vast memorabilia room. It contained a little of everything rare and valuable in the world. Original Warhols and Banksys lined one wall. Others were teeming with first-edition books, signed footballs, baseballs, framed jerseys. Egyptian and Native American artifacts, all stolen and sold on the black market, anchored one corner.

In the center of it all was a million-dollar record collection, filled with mint-condition first pressings of the entire history of modern music: the Beatles, the Stones, Pink Floyd, Nirvana, Public Enemy, it was all accounted for. On a high shelf was the third Martel record, with its blood red label and a stenciled number three, on a pedestal in a locked glass case. A small spotlight was positioned perfectly to bathe it in warm, inviting light.

Brick stared at the record. "All this fuss over that?"

"One of the rarest records in the world," Ray replied.

"No one's getting past me, boss. You know that. Why don't you get some rest?"

"Any word on Watts yet?"

"He's still not answering his phone. I got a buddy driving to Philly, checking in on him first thing in the morning."

Ray slammed his glass of whisky. "I'm putting it in the safe, just to be sure."

Ray swung one of the Warhols open, revealing a wall-safe behind it. There was a loud bang in the living room. Ray flinched, half-ducked, his coke paranoia in full swing. "What the fuck was that!?"

"Probably just more birds, sir. They keep running into the windows. I have a message into building management."

Ray rubbed his chest, breathing deeply. "Goddamnit! The money I pay for this place! Fucking birds?"

Outside, a spiral of crows flew higher and higher, squawking louder and louder, their eyes black holes squinting through the tempered glass.

Side C: Track 3: Massacre on the 50th Floor (4:39)

1.

Nina had never been to New York City. Even under the current circumstances, it was a thrill. The towering skyscrapers, the bustling corner bodegas, the throngs of people from all over the world choking the sidewalks. Detroit was a big city, no doubt, but New York was different, a singular vibe all its own. Just the thought of all the incredible record stores hidden amongst its streets gave her chills. She vowed to make it back there, in better times, and with some money in her pocket.

Killian drove through Harlem before circling around the perimeter of Central Park. He managed to find street parking within eyesight of Ray's high-rise, a true miracle. They stared at the glass and steel monstrosity before them. The building stuck out like a sore thumb, modern, but already somehow dated, the cheap construction tucked in between established, old-school brick apartment buildings and businesses.

"Of course, that's where he lives," Nina said, annoyed.

"A champion of gentrification, I see."

"Oh, absolutely. He probably tore down an entire block of history, and built this piece of shit himself."

Killian opened his door, "Well, let's see how far we can get."

2.

Ray stood before his wall of glass, a petty king of no one, staring at the lights of the skyline circling Central Park. Occasionally, a screeching crow would pass a few feet from the window. The glass was littered with smudges, a few tufts of feathers, several spots of blood. Ray inhaled harshly through his nose every few seconds, his septum long gone. He'd not slept in days.

Brick was at the dining room table, scrolling through his phone, stifling a yawn. A security screen on the wall lit up, the building concierge coming through a speaker. "Sir, so sorry to bother you again, but they refuse to leave the lobby without speaking to you first. Would you like me to phone the police?"

"Fuck!" Ray yelled. He slammed his fist on the glass, glaring at Brick. "Do your fucking job, man!"

Nina and Killian waited in the lobby, standing on a polished marble floor, surrounded by obnoxiously white furniture. The building concierge, an older gentleman in a suit hiding behind a large monitor, gave them the stink eye. The elevator dinged, and Brick loomed over them.

"Sir, it's very important that we speak to Mr. Wise, right away," Killian said.

"That's just not happening," Brick replied.

"He is in grave danger."

"That's why I'm here. That's what Mr. Wise pays me for."

"People are dying!" Nina interjected. The concierge perked up at this, raising his eyebrows.

"Mr. Wise is well aware of that fact."

"He knows?" Nina asked.

"Mr. Wise is a very careful man. He was very sorry to hear about your father. He only wishes he had taken him up on his most generous offer. Maybe then, all this nasty business could have been avoided."

Nina stepped towards Brick, furious, "So, it's my father's own fault that he's dead? You tell that little fucking prick..."

Killian stepped in between them, holding Nina back. "I apologize for my colleague, Sir. Is there any chance I could speak to Mr. Wise, alone, face to face? Just for a few minutes?"

"Afraid not. We have to be extra careful, given the current circumstances. No offense, Father, but I'm sure you understand."

"You tell him he needs a priest more than he needs a bodyguard right now, *no offense*. You don't know what the hell you're dealing with!" Nina yelled.

"I think it's time for you to leave." Brick said.

"I agree!" The concierge added.

"We're not going any..." Killian grabbed Nina by the arm, leading her towards the exit before she could finish. Nina shrugged off his hand, "You're just giving up?"

"We're not getting past him right now, no thanks to you."

Nina yelled over her shoulder. "Tell him Henry Watts is dead too, and he's next!"

Brick's smug smirk faded from his face. As they passed through the revolving glass doors, the concierge added. "I will call the police if you step foot in here again. This lobby is for residents only!" Satisfied, he went back to his security monitor.

3.

Ray paced even faster.

"Watts too? Maybe we should get out of the city."

"No one's getting in here," Brick replied.

"I think I'd feel better at one of the beach houses. Should I call the copter?"

"Trust me, boss. This is the safest place to be right now. The alarm's set, we're locked down tight. We're inside a steel fortress, and the drawbridge is up, okay?"

"Okay, okay." Ray used a credit card to sift through a pile of blow, breaking off a large line.

"Sir, again, with all due respect, maybe it's time to lay off for a bit? Why don't you try and get some shuteye? I've got a pot of coffee going for myself, and I'm not going anywhere."

Ray stared at him. He didn't like being told what to do, but Brick had a point. "You're right, you're right," he begrudgingly admitted. Ray put the credit card down and reached for a bottle of whiskey.

4.

Downstairs, Nina and Killian sat in the car, devouring massive slices of pepperoni pizza. Most of the building was dark, except for the penthouse, still glowing yellow at the top. Nina wiped her chin with a napkin. "Damn, you were not wrong about this."

"Told you, best pizza in New York," Killian said.

"When all this is over, I'm taking you to my spot back home. You can experience some O.G. Detroit-style deep dish. It's even better than this." Killian raised an eyebrow. "But this is a close second, don't get me wrong!"

"I'll have to take you up on that."

Nina scoped out the building again, looking for anything out of the ordinary. "Maybe we'll get lucky. Maybe he'll use the elevator this time."

"Just pray he doesn't come tonight. Maybe we, no, maybe *I,* can reason with Mr. Wise in the light of day. He has to leave this place eventually."

"Good luck with that. Surprised he didn't have us thrown in jail already."

"Me too, after what you pulled."

"C'mon. His henchman was being a royal prick."

They continued to eat in silence. Nina studied Killian. "You ever get lonely?"

"Lonely?" Killian set his slice on a grease-coated paper plate.

"Yeah, choosing this life, the whole celibacy thing?"

"I didn't really choose it, to be honest."

"What do you mean?"

"My parents both worked for the church, two of my sisters are nuns, one of my younger brothers is on his way to being a Cardinal."

"How many siblings do you have?"

"Five."

"Five? You really are Catholic."

"And my big brother was the black sheep, in and out of jail, bar fights, drunk driving, forced into the military by a judge. I was second in line, so the pressure fell squarely on me to make up for his indiscretions."

"But you didn't want to?"

"I did, at first. But a long time ago, I made the decision to walk away from all of it."

"Why?"

"A woman, an amazing woman."

"It's always a woman, isn't it? What happened? Why didn't you?"

Killian sighed, threw up his arms. "All of this."

"So, you're telling me you chose cold pizza and demon records over love?"

"Something like that."

"Do you know what happened to her?"

"I looked her up a few times. She opened up a pediatric clinic in Illinois."

"You ever reach out?"

"She's happily married, retired, enjoying her grandkids. She doesn't want to hear from me."

"I'm sorry."

"Don't be. I'm happy for her. It took me a long time to get there, but I'm at peace with it. At least most of the time. How about you? How are you doing?"

"Better than you, apparently."

Killian laughed. "Has it hit you yet, your father? You lost your mom too, right?"

Nina stared at her lap. "Cancer."

"That's tough."

"You have no idea."

"I lost both my parents, in my thirties."

"Really? What happened?"

"Car accident."

"Does it ever get any easier?"

"No, not really. But the pain, the anger, they lessen over time."

"I still can't believe they're both gone."

"I liken grief to a hardening of the soul. You have to develop a callus, in a way, to deal with the loss, to accept it, truly, in your heart."

"I think that's a long way out for me."

"It is, but you'll get there. Trust me, I did. And when you emerge on the other side, you'll be stronger."

Nina held back tears.

"What about your personal life? You have a boyfriend you can lean on?" Killian asked.

"There was, a girlfriend, but I messed it all up."

Killian nodded.

"Does that bother you? Me being gay?"

"No, not at all. If women make you happy, then I'm happy for you."

"I have to say, you are one of the most empathetic men of faith I have ever met."

"Unfortunately, that's a very true statement. We're far too rare these days."

5.

Ray woke up in bed. He had actually fallen asleep for a few hours. His mouth tasted like rancid sand, and he reached for the wine fridge next to his bed. The fridge was dark, the familiar otherworldly glow from behind the glass was gone. He opened it, the bottled French water inside was half-warm. Ray's blood boiled. Twenty million dollars, and he still had to worry about goddamn power outages? He sat up in bed. "Brick? What the hell?"

There was no response, only a muffled thump from somewhere deep in the penthouse. "Brick?" Still nothing. "Useless fuck," Ray mumbled to himself. His hands shook as he crept to his bedroom door. He swung it open slowly, the hallway ahead of him pitch-black.

***

Nina's head hit the passenger window, waking her up. The entire building was black. She shook Killian awake.

"What? What?" Killian asked woozily.

"The whole place is dark!"

Nina and Killian raced across the street. Inside the lobby, the concierge fumbled with a flashlight, checking a fuse box panel. He swiveled around when the handicap door opened, shining the beam in their eyes. "No way, not you two again. Are you behind this?" He came out from behind the counter, attempting a defiant stance.

Nina decked him, hard.

"Nina!" Killian gasped.

The concierge flopped to the floor. Nina grabbed his flashlight and handed it to Killian. "We don't have time to deal with his bullshit!" Nina ran ahead, searching for the stairway.

***

Ray crept down the hallway, his cellphone light barely piercing the darkness. "Brick? Where the hell are you?" It came out as a strained whisper, weak. The floor to ceiling windows in the living room let in the deep blue glow from the city lights below. His stomach lurched, and he turned off his light. He had already seen too much of the carnage in front of him.

The walls and glass were covered in blood. Brick sat at the dining room table, his head no longer on his shoulders. Instead, it rested on the tabletop, a macabre centerpiece. Brick's bulging eyes stared at Ray in the dark, blood dripping from the table onto the bamboo floors. Ray slowly backed away, a trembling hand over his mouth, stifling a scream.

***

Nina took the steps two at a time, but she was slowing down. Her breath was ragged, and sweat ran down her forehead. She stopped and peered over the railing. Killian was at least ten floors below her, hobbling up as fast as he could. He looked up, "Go! I'm right behind you!" She pushed on.

***

Ray hit the hallway, turning his back on the horror and sprinting for the front door. As soon as his hand felt the lock, he knew something was wrong. He turned on his flashlight. The deadbolt was twisted, bent, as if it had been melted into the doorframe by a blowtorch. He yanked on the handle; it wouldn't budge. He banged on the door with both hands, "Help! Anyone? Help!"

There was only silence, then banging from the other side. Ray jumped from the sound. It was Nina, breathing hard. "Hey! You okay in there?"

"I can't get out, the door's fucked!"

Nina scanned the dark hallway, bathed in a glowing red from the Exit signs along the corridor. She eyed a fire extinguisher. "Hold on!"

"Hurry! There's someone in here with me!"

"No shit! You stupid bastard! Hold on!"

Nina yanked the extinguisher from the wall and went to town on the door, bashing it over and over again. The doorknob gradually loosened, the lock bending, slowly giving away as the door frame began to splinter.

Ray stood back, watching the door bend inward from the blows. "Hurry!" Behind him, a rope slithered down the hallway, silent, stalking its prey. The rope wrapped tightly around Ray's ankle. "Something's on me!" The rope went taut, yanking Ray onto his back, his head slamming into the door as he went down, opening a gash in his scalp.

The rope dragged Ray kicking and screaming through the penthouse, leaving behind a trail of blood from his leaking head. His journey ended in the library, at ManDown's feet. ManDown towered over him, fire burning in his eyes. There was no shirt beneath his hoodie, the ropes twisting around his raw, exposed flesh, moving in and out of multiple wounds on his body. The Warhol was ripped in half on the floor, Ray's safe exposed. ManDown squatted, his face close to Ray's, "Open it."

Ray responded in a high-pitched whine, "You can't do this. Do you know who the fuck I am?"

ManDown flipped Ray over onto his stomach. Ray squealed as ManDown shoved his hand between his shoulder blades, melting through them, upwards, his hand following his spine, up his neck, burrowing into Ray's skull. Ray stopped screaming, his body convulsing. ManDown's middle and ring fingers emerged from behind Ray's eyeballs, forcing them out of his head. They dropped onto the plush carpet below, a puddle of fluid. ManDown's thumb exited Ray's mouth, gripping his upper teeth, his head a human bowling ball.

ManDown stood, bringing Ray's body up with him, controlling him like a puppet. Ray shambled to the safe, a bleeding marionette with twitching limbs. Ray raised one hand, clumsily entering the combination. Once the safe clicked open, ManDown yanked his hand out. Ray slumped to the floor, a pile of meat. ManDown wiped Ray's brains on the hem of his bathrobe, and kicked the corpse aside.

6.

Nina was nearly through the door when Killian arrived at her side. He propped himself against the wall, his body in pain. "He's here," Nina told him.

Killian nodded, unable to speak.

With one last blow, the extinguisher splintered the wood, and Nina kicked the door open. She bolted inside.

"Wait!" Killian wheezed. Nina raced down the hallway. Killian limped after her, "Be careful!"

Nina burst through the doorway of the library. ManDown stood over Ray's corpse, the third record already in his hands. Black, shadowy snakes emanated from the record, encircling his arm, weaving themselves into the rope, seeking out the open wounds in his flesh. His eyes were white with a fire so bright it burned her retinas.

"You're too late," ManDown growled, his voice deep, loud, echoing.

Behind him, a doorway appeared out of the shadows, his bunker on the other side. Nina could see Henry's corpse, disemboweled, covered in insects. Nina closed her eyes and rushed him, raising the dented extinguisher over her head. She brought it down with all the strength she had left within her.

The extinguisher bounced off him like he was a statue made of granite. Pain shuddered through Nina's hands, and the extinguisher fell to the floor. ManDown gripped Nina by her throat with his free hand, lifting her high into the air. Nina gasped, choking, kicking at him uselessly.

His fingers burned intensely, and Nina felt his fingertips melt through her skin, slipping beneath her flesh. Once they were inside her body, the room disappeared, her vision going black. In the darkness, the triplets laughed.

***

When her vision returned, she was in the triplets' bedroom, her body paralyzed, pressed tight against the wall. The triplets were in their beds just a few feet away from her, still three normal children, blissfully asleep.

Outside, a storm approached the farmhouse, thunder rumbling in the distance, bolts of lightning crackling in the sky. A cool breeze blew through the open window, extinguishing a single candle burning on a nightstand. A crow flew down from the storm, fluttering above the windowsill before landing on it, its black claws gripping the wood.

Beneath the wind, Nina could just make out some sort of faint chanting coming from outside. A shadow darkened the window, blacker than the night sky. An arm-like appendage of smoke stretched forth from it with long black fingers, seeping into the girls' room, floating towards their bed. As it passed through the crow, the bird let out a frightened squawk, before falling to the floor, dead.

The shadow wrapped itself around the neck of the sister closest to the window. She bolted awake, the icy grip around her tiny throat silencing her screams. The smoky claws pried her mouth open, and the shadow forced its way down her gullet. She writhed in pain before going still, her back stiff as a board. When she opened her eyes, they were black pools.

The girl twisted her head towards Nina. Her limbs unlocked, and she flipped onto her stomach. Rising up on all fours, she climbed from the bed onto the wall, moving up the crumbling plaster like a spider, crawling onto the ceiling.

The girl's eyes remained fixed on Nina's as she hung upside down. She opened her mouth, "Why are you here?"

Nina tried to speak, but nothing came out.

"Why are you here?" The girl screamed as she rushed towards her, scuttling across the attic ceiling on her hands and knees. She leapt onto Nina, clawing at her face.

***

Killian staggered into the room. "Stop!" ManDown turned his burning eyes slowly upon him.

"Stop!" Killian bellowed again. Though at times his faith had wavered, now he stood a pillar against the darkness before him. "You three-faced demons, possessors of children, violators and accursed. Heed my words! In the name of the Father, Son, and Holy Spirit, I commit thee to perdition..." Killian sprang forward and shook holy water on him, dousing ManDown's face and chest with the blessed liquid. ManDown's skin sizzled and blistered. He staggered back, dropping Nina to the floor.

As soon as the contact was broken between them, Nina was back in the penthouse. She crawled away, gasping for air, feeling her neck for wounds. Killian shook more holy water on him, soaking his chest, the ropes. ManDown stumbled back, hunching over. He closed his eyes, taking deep breaths. As he did so, his skin recovered, the blisters repairing themselves, the ropes scraping away the scabs from his body onto the floor. ManDown opened his flaming eyes again, smiling at Killian. He held up the record. "It's too late, old man. It's already over."

ManDown shuffled towards the doorway. Killian dove after him, falling to his knees, gripping ManDown's wrist. Killian dug his fingernails into his hand, trying to pry the record from his grasp. Shadowy tendrils attacked Killian, striking his arms, burning his flesh. He yelled in agony, letting go. Smoke rose from his charred flesh.

Killian drew out his book from his coat, searching for a passage. ManDown snatched it out of his hands, threw it on the floor.

"Enough lies. Let me show you the truth." ManDown grabbed Killian by an ankle and dragged him towards the doorway. ManDown was crossing the threshold when Nina made it back to her feet.

"No! Stop!" Nina screamed.

Killian was only halfway through, his waist lying on the threshold of the doorway. ManDown stared at Nina, grinning. "Okay."

The doorway closed. ManDown was gone, as were Killian's legs. Only his upper body was left in the room, half of his intestines exposed, blackened, steaming on the carpet.

7.

"No, no, no, no!" Nina rushed to Killian, cradling his head and shoulders in her lap.

Killian blinked rapidly, shock taking over his body. He surveyed his lower half, what was left of it, and attempted a chuckle. "That's not good."

"Shh," Nina whispered.

"It's okay, Nina. It's okay." Killian coughed, blood trickling from his mouth.

Nina rocked him gently. "Quiet now. Save your strength."

"There are things you need to know. Things I should have told you."

"Shh."

Killian coughed again. "This happened once before. The three records, used in tandem. The three demons, once they're together again, inside him, they can open a doorway."

"A doorway? To where?"

"To the other side."

"What?"

"To the darkness. You, you must stop him. It could be the end of everything, if he's successful, if he lets them through…" Killian coughed up more blood. Nina wiped it away with her sleeve. "He'll have to use a holy site for the final ritual, a church, or something similar, something sacred, it must be the ultimate subversion of God. Look for the signs, the crows, the…" Killian's chest shook, his skin ghostly white, a large pool of blood encircling them. "You won't have much time, I'm afraid, now that he has all three."

"I can't do this. Not without you!"

"You can. And I'm sorry I failed you. I'm sorry that the burden must fall on you."

Killian closed his eyes. Nina was silent, waiting for him to pass, rocking him gently. His eyes burst open again, a last gasp. "Maybe you were right, Nina."

"Shh. It's okay. Don't talk."

"Maybe we were wrong to try and contain this, to try and keep it hidden under lock and key." Killian struggled to focus, his dying brain trying to formulate its last thought. "Destroying the records, all the copies, and now his growing power, that could explain it."

"Wait, how do you mean?"

Killian didn't respond. His body went limp, his last breath expelling from his lips. Nina sobbed, pressed her forehead into his.

8.

Nina was surprised by how quiet the university was as she crept from shadow to shadow in the middle of the night. Then she remembered that if these students were engaging in any sinful activities, they were probably doing so in secrecy. She doubted that there was a Frat-row on this campus.

Nina used Killian's keys and his ID badge to circumvent the library security system. She opened the secret archives door and took in its varied contents. She reached up on her tiptoes, grabbing the crate containing the original set of records. She opened a glass case and removed an ancient shroud of some sort from inside. She used it to wipe the blood and ants from the records, then tossed it on the floor.

Nina left the door to the archives wide-open, and all the lights on inside. She wasn't keeping anyone's secrets for them.

In the parking lot, Nina sat behind the wheel of Killian's car for a long time. The records sat on the passenger seat, beads of blood still oozing from them. Nina had both hands on the wheel, her eyes closed. She took in deep breaths, attempting to calm herself down, trying to figure out what to do. She thought about what Killian had said at the end, what it might mean.

Nina started the car, put it into gear, and drove off into the night.

Side C: Interlude 3: They Just Tore That Poor Man Apart (3:44)

The following is a transcript of a police interview conducted on May 6th, 1943, in the Portland, Maine police station. The detective in charge of the investigation was Albert Manning, a self-proclaimed technophile who spent his nights and weekends building radios and fixing his neighbor's televisions.

Detective Manning was an early adopter of wire recorders, a portable device that could record sound onto hair-thin steel wires. In fact, he was one of the only law enforcement professionals in the United States at the time to use such technology out in the field.

Any text in italics is opinion rather than fact, added later by Detective Manning as he typed up this interview for inclusion into his case files.

The subject of the interview is one Alexander Cahill, 22 years old, a graduating senior from St. John's Catholic University Seminary.

This is the only official record of any kind related to the Martel triplet's exorcism.

MANNING: You okay, son? Sorry to keep you cooped up in here for so long, and sorry for how the fellas were treating you before I got here.

Subject is paranoid, out of it. He keeps checking the door, the one-way mirror, his left eye twitches erratically.

MANNING: Take some deep breaths now. You're safe here, and you're in good hands with me. Can I get you more coffee, some water?

CAHILL: No, no thank you.

Subject seems to see the cup of coffee sitting before him, now cold, for the first time. He takes a long drink.

MANNING: Now, like I said. Those boys outside the door were treating you like a suspect as I understand it, and that is just not the case, okay? I want to be very clear on that. And I want you to know that I am a God-fearing Catholic myself, life-long, and I have nothing but respect for you and the cloth. So, you can tell me the truth, cause I'll believe you. I was in that room myself, before coming here, and I sure as hell felt it. That was the work of the devil, and I'll contest anyone that claims different. Far as I'm concerned, this here's an open and shut case. I just need to dot my Is and cross my Ts. Alright, son? Let's get this done and get you home.

CAHILL: Thank you. I'd like that.

Subject's shoulders seem to drop, a release of tension, his breathing normal.

MANNING: So, how many of these exorcisms have you been involved with?

CAHILL: This was my fifth.

MANNING: All with Father Chabot?

CAHILL: Correct.

MANNING: What can you tell me about him?

CAHILL: Father Phillip Chabot? He is, or was, rather, the world's most renowned exorcist. He's one of the most important men in the entire Catholic church.

MANNING: Had anything similar to this ever happened previously? Did you ever feel like you were in danger? Feel that the victims were in danger?

CAHILL: No. The complete opposite in fact. Father Chabot truly helped people. He saved lives, he saved souls, hundreds of them, likely thousands. I left our previous sessions elated, spiritually full. To watch that man work was a dream come true. I had studied him for years, you know, his methods, before meeting him in person. There's a reason he was considered the best. To see him in action, before he retired, it was an honor.

MANNING: Was that his plan? To retire?

CAHILL: It was. Doing what he did, it takes a toll. That's why the church wanted to preserve his ways, his methods.

MANNING: And that's where you came in. You've been recording them, with a gramophone?

CAHILL: Nothing like what you have here.

The subject motions towards my wire recorder, clearly impressed.

CAHILL: The church is a little behind the times I'm afraid, but records are still the easiest way for us to mass-produce, to distribute to our seminaries around the world.

MANNING: Are you familiar with the reel-to-reel magnetic recorders?

CAHILL: Yes! I've been reading up on them in Popular Mechanics. My hope is, or was, to lobby for those by next year.

MANNING: I would sure like to get my hands on one myself. Why did you say *was*, as in past tense?

CAHILL: Well, I imagine last night was the end of the program.

MANNING: Okay, take me through last night. Let's start with where you were.

There was a long silence, his fear and anxiety returning at the mere mention of the previous night.

CAHILL: We arrived at the Martel farm just after lunch.

MANNING: For the record, the farm located just outside of Readfield, correct?

CAHILL: Correct. We met with the family briefly, prayed with them, and then asked the parents to leave the home.

MANNING: Was that standard procedure?

CAHILL: Yes, Father Chabot insisted on an empty home, clear from any external, potentially negative forces.

MANNING: Negative forces?

CAHILL: It's very rare that an entire family is truly accepting of us, or even believes that a true possession is occurring in their home, even when they're practicing Catholics. Father Chabot was sensitive to the darkness of suspicion, of non-believers. He felt it clouded his mind, affected his work in a negative way. Freeing the house of that allowed him to focus on the only darkness that truly mattered.

MANNING: How were the parents yesterday?

CAHILL: To be honest, the father seemed a little off.

MANNING: Abraham Martel? How so?

CAHILL: He didn't seem, how do I say it? He was very matter of fact about everything. He didn't seem to be surprised at all or frightened by what was happening to his daughters. In fact, he seemed more irritated that his wife had bothered to contact the church. As if what was happening to his daughters was no worse than a cold, something that would pass on its own. And let me tell you, it was anything but. There was an evil in that house like none I have ever experienced.

MANNING: Worse than your previous sessions? Aside from the obvious, I mean.

CAHILL: Something was different yesterday. I'm still new to this, but I felt true evil myself, deep inside my bones, for the first time. A darkness weighed on me, heavily. At first, I thought it was just me, but even Father Chabot was quieter than usual, and short-tempered as we got things ready, really agitated. I could tell it weighed on him as well.

MANNING: What happened next?

Silence again, the subject begins to cry. I pass him my handkerchief.

CAHILL: We went into the girls' bedroom, I set everything up, and began recording, the usual routine.

MANNING: The girls, meaning the triplets?

CAHILL: Correct. Abigail, Annie, and Arlene Martel.

The subject breaks down even more after saying the victims' names, an audible sob.

CAHILL: It was quickly clear to Chabot that this was not going to be a routine exorcism.

MANNING: Is there such a thing as a routine exorcism?

CAHILL: For him, after how many he had done, there actually was, but this was not one of them. In Germany, many years back, he had dealt with identical twins that had been possessed by a single demon, and he assumed that's what this was. He soon realized that we were dealing with three demons, three very powerful demons, possessing three sisters at the same time. Now to be clear, this has never been known to occur before yesterday.

MANNING: Explain to me what you saw. What symptoms were the girls displaying?

CAHILL: Their father had tied them down with ropes to their beds. According to their mother, they had been climbing the walls and ceiling. As we got underway, the ropes seemed to come alive, moving on their own, under some sort of control. The girls' beds began lifting into the air and slamming down onto the floor repeatedly. Their skin blistered, their eyes burned with fire, and they spoke in languages they could not possibly have known. And worse, they spoke a foul language so ancient Father Chabot did not even know of it. Even after all his years in the field, he had no idea what it was.

MANNING: Had that ever happened before, in your experience?

CAHILL: Never. This was the first time I witnessed Father Chabot show any hesitation at all in a room, let alone fear. He seemed to think he might be out of his depth. I believe, maybe, for the first time in his career, for the first time in his life.

MANNING: What happened next?

CAHILL: He began the ritual. The rites, the readings, the holy water, the sign of the cross. Only, nothing worked. It only made things worse, escalating everything. The demons seemed to be feeding off everything Chabot tried. The windows exploded, as did the lights in the room. Furniture moved on its own, smashing against the wall, splintering into pieces.

MANNING: And the girls?

CAHILL: They were in total agony, screaming in terror, trying to fight what was inside them. They would lose the battle, and these deep, raw voices would erupt from their tiny frames, loud enough to make my ears ring. They're ringing still, in fact.

The subject went quiet again. More sobs.

MANNING: What happened next?

CAHILL: Those girls, those innocent little girls, they just tore that poor man apart!

MANNING: And what did you do?

CAHILL: I ran. I ran as fast as I could!

The subject breaks down completely at this point, ashamed, inconsolable. I give him a minute to compose himself.

MANNING: Where are the records now, the recordings you made? I'd like to hear them.

CAHILL: I don't think you want to do that.

MANNING: No, I don't think that I do, but I need to corroborate your story, so I can clear you.

CAHILL: Clear me? You said I wasn't a suspect?

MANNING: I assure, son, you are not. Like I said, just dotting my Is, and crossing my...

At this point we were interrupted by Officer Leary. An attorney for the subject had arrived at the station, sent by the church. An expensive suit out of New York. He demanded to see his client at once, and I obliged. I plan to continue this interview at a later date and will update this record accordingly.

Detective Albert Manning

May 6th, 1943, 11:18 AM

Portland, Maine - Case # 3043

There is no record of Detective Manning ever being able to successfully locate or communicate further with Father Cahill after May 6th. At least officially, this interview was never concluded, and

Detective Manning was never able to recover the recordings made the previous night.

{flip the record}

Side D: Track 1: Two Homecomings, Two Plans (5:03)

1.

Maggie sat in the broadcast booth at 89.3, Rap-City Radio, the only hip-hop station left in Detroit not yet bought out by the conglomerates. She eyed the clock, looking forward to the end of her shift. She spoke into her mic with a smooth, effortless voice. "Alright peeps. One more from me, and then DJ Stacks takes the wheel. As always, thanks for letting me ride with you."

Maggie turned a knob, slowly raising the volume on Gang Starr's 'DWYCK.' She removed her headphones and packed up her things. DJ Stacks entered the booth, sipping on a coffee. "Ending with a stone-cold classic. How am I supposed to follow this up?"

"That's just it, you can't!"

"Every night you do this to me!"

"You love the challenge."

"Hot date tonight?"

Maggie gave him a dirty look. "You know the answer to that. See ya tomorrow, Stacks."

It was an unseasonably cool night as Maggie exited the station, an old brick building on the edge of downtown. She rolled the sleeves of her hoodie down. Ear buds in, she searched her phone for the perfect playlist as she headed down the sidewalk.

Halfway down the block, Maggie turned around. She felt like someone was watching her. Sure enough, ten yards behind her, a dark figure emerged from under a streetlight, bathed in shadow. Maggie turned and picked up her pace, hurrying towards the busy intersection ahead. She swung her backpack around to her chest, fishing in the outer pocket for her mace. She was almost to the cross street when a hand gripped her shoulder. Maggie spun around, ready to fight.

"Maggie! It's me!" Nina cried, stepping back, raising her hands in the air.

Maggie yanked her ear buds out of her ears. "Jesus, Nina! What the fuck?"

"I'm sorry! I was calling your name."

"You can't just follow another woman down a dark street at night! You're lucky I didn't soak you with this thing." Maggie held up her mace.

Nina dropped her eyes, bursting into tears, "I'm sorry, for real. I just, I really need your help. I don't have anyone else."

Maggie was shocked by the show of emotion from Nina. She had never seen her shed a single tear when they were together. Maggie knew immediately that this, whatever it was, was real, not just some cheap ploy to win her back. Nina looked exhausted, thin. She had large bags under her eyes and bruises on her neck. Maggie placed a hand on Nina's shoulder. "It's okay, it's okay. What's wrong? What's going on?"

2.

St. Michael's Catholic school had seen better days, and it hadn't seen those days in a long time. Its enrollment peaked in the eighties, its halls and classrooms packed with children. After that, the changing neighborhood, and the erosion of faith in America, led to a steady decline in students. By the time the recession hit in 2008, the school was forced to close and had been abandoned ever since.

Now, it was a merely a crumbling relic of another era, surrounded by a tall, barb-wire fence. The fence hadn't really done its job, and the school building was covered with graffiti, most of its windows shattered. The chapel that stood in the school's shadow was in similar shape. It was still an impressive piece of architecture, even with much of its stone façade covered in spray paint, and many of its stained-glass windows broken, pigeons fluttering in and out.

ManDown stood on the other side of the fence, staring at the buildings, which took up their own block of a mostly uninhabited neighborhood. As he did so, a murder of crows took off from the roof of the school. A few landed on the chapel, and the others continued to fly, forming a tight funnel above the chapel's lone steeple. ManDown breathed in the fresh air.

It was perfect.

Behind him stood a dozen men and women, all homeless. ManDown nodded his head in satisfaction. His followers stepped forward, moving slowly, their eyes unfocused, their minds no longer their own. A man used a bolt-cutter on the fence, snipping the links from top to bottom. He pried each side back, creating a jagged oval.

The man's palms bled as he held the serrated fence open for ManDown to pass. The others followed behind, carrying speakers, turntables, dollies strapped with large generators, bundles of long, industrial extension cords. The oldest of the crew, a woman nearing eighty, went through last. She only carried two things, a hammer, and a machete. Ants swarmed in each footprint she left in the sandy soil.

3.

Even with everything that had happened, Nina was glad to be home, glad to be back in her father's store. It still felt surreal though, being there without him, like she was in some poorly built recreation of Round-A-Bout-Reggie's on a sound stage somewhere. The store was dark, hot, and musty, a layer of dust already settling over everything.

Since her father opened the place, this was the longest it had ever stood closed. Reggie would open for at least a few hours every single day, even on holidays, giving the local outcasts a much-needed refuge from their stressful family gatherings. A few customers that had grown up and went off to college would always stop by if they were back in town, and Reggie would beam with pride as they told him stories about the hidden vinyl gems they had found in their new cities. A few customers had even gone on to open their own shops, and would seek Reggie out for advice, which he was always happy to supply. Nina tried to put all of that out of her mind, she had already done more than enough crying.

"You sure about this?" Maggie asked.

Nina looked down at herself. She was strapped to a chair in the center of the store, her father's leather belts tied around her arms and legs. A pair of headphones hung around her neck, connected to an antique turntable. The original copy of the first record sat upon it. "Hell no. Definitely not sure about this."

"What if you become, like, possessed or something?"

"It didn't affect my dad like that."

"That doesn't mean shit. You think it's hereditary, how it affects you?"

"If anything happens, St. Agnes is what, three blocks from here? Just run over there and grab a priest."

"Nina! C'mon. This is serious!"

"I know it is, but I have no choice. Thank you for believing me."

Maggie sighed. "Jury's still out on that, but I'm trying."

Nina took a few deep breaths, clearing her head. "Alright. I'm ready. Do it."

"You sure?"

Nina nodded. Maggie lifted up the headphones, securing them to Nina's ears, making sure they were tight. She raised the needle on the turntable, and gently set it down into the outer groove. She stepped back like she had just lit a fuse on some fireworks.

"No matter what, just let it play. I need to be sure I can handle it." Nina smiled at Maggie and closed her eyes. Static filled her ears, bouncing around her head. Beneath the static, dead tongues whispered, then screamed...

***

... and it was 1943, and Nina was back in the farmhouse outside of Readfield, Maine. She was back in the upstairs bedroom, pressed against the wall. This time, it felt like she was experiencing her surroundings on old, deteriorating film, run through a half-broken projector. Everything was just out of focus, all bleeding colors and jerking motions. She squinted, trying to see the triplets more clearly, even though they were only a few feet away.

The triplets were strapped to their beds, screaming in terror, flames shooting from their inky black eyes, scorching the skin on their cheeks and foreheads. Father Chabot towered over them, soaking them with holy water. The ropes twisted around the girls as their skin blistered from the water, peeling away in strips. The ropes wormed their way inside the girls through tiny open wounds in their skin.

Alexander Cahill, terrified, monitored the gramophone in the corner, its horn-like funnel pointed at the beds. The turntable slowly spun, recording, its needle etching record #3. He kept his back to the proceedings, focusing on the record, clutching a rosary against his chest, mumbling a prayer over and over. His body visibly buckled with fear.

On the wall adjacent to Alexander, Nina could see something small, circular, inside a knot in the wood paneling. It caught the light from the window and reflected it back at her, flickering. Whatever it was, she couldn't make it out.

"I cast you out! I cast you out you vile monsters, you abhorrent abominations! Begone! This is God's house now, and you are no longer welcome!" Chabot shouted at them, trying to be heard over the demonic screams and chants rising from the girls. They were ear-splitting in the small room. The beds buckled, then rose off the floor. They hovered there, the ropes spinning around the girls and their bedframes, tightening, loosening, then tightening again, allowing them to breathe, then cutting off their oxygen, strangling them.

"I command you, in the name of the Holy Father, begone!"

Chabot threw more holy water on them, and the beds crashed down. A silence filled the room. A lamp in the corner came back on, bathing the room in a warm light. The triplets began to cry. Their ropes were suddenly slack, loose around their bodies. Their features softened, their skin clearing up. They looked like normal, scared little girls. They spoke together, almost in unison, "What happened? Where are we? Where's mother?" Their voices were once again their own, high-pitched, whiny.

Father Chabot rushed to them, tears streaming down his face. "It'll be okay girls, it's over, you're safe now. The Lord Jesus Christ has prevailed." He untied the ropes, throwing them onto the floor. The triplets grinned, stealing mischievous glances amongst themselves. Nina saw the faint flicker of flames reflecting in their eyes. Nina tried to speak, to warn him, but she was paralyzed within the vision, mute, helpless...

***

...Inside Round-A-Bout-Reggie's, Nina grimaced in pain, twitching in her chair, pulling against her restraints. The record was spinning faster and faster, the lights in the store flickering. Maggie paced back and forth, trying to ignore what was happening. She couldn't take any more. She reached for the headphone cord. Nina, her eyes still closed, gasped, "No! Not yet. Let it play, let it play." Maggie shook her head, cracked her knuckles, and went back to her pacing...

***

...As Father Chabot comforted the triplets, the ropes on the floor moved once again, silently preparing to strike him. Nina tried again to scream a warning, even though she knew this was the past, even though she knew it would do nothing to change the course of events that she was witnessing. A single rope slithered around Chabot's leg, wrenching him to the floor. As the other ropes rose up, the triplets' bodies tightened. They became rigid, flat as boards on the mattresses. Flames shot from their eyes once again.

The ropes attacked Chabot, gripping his limbs, and raising him up into the air, above the girls. "Help me!" Chabot choked. Alexander only backed away sobbing, his mouth hanging open. He collapsed in the corner, burying his face in his knees, whimpering a prayer to himself. The ropes twisted Chabot's body, contorting it, tearing muscle, bringing his pained face within inches of the triplets.' They cackled, deep and raspy, a sandpaper scream.

"We cast *you* out, you vile monster! Begone!" The triplets roared in unison.

The ropes pulled in all directions at once, like horses goaded to dismember a criminal. Chabot was torn into pieces, his arms and legs flying across the room, his blood and organs showering down upon the girls. The triplets, drenched in his crimson viscera, kept laughing, louder and louder. The gramophone kept recording, kept spinning, faster and faster, the record now soaked in Chabot's blood, the needle etching the blood into the grooves. Static filled the room. Alexander fled down the stairs screaming.

The triplets all swung their heads in unison towards Nina, their flaming eyes seeing her for the first time. They rose from their beds, floating in the air, the ropes carrying them towards her. Nina squirmed, trying to free herself from the vision. The triplets hovered inches from her face, staring deep into Nina's eyes. Nina could smell the blood dripping down their cheeks, the coppery aroma burning her nostrils. Nina felt their silent gaze infecting her soul, filling it with a profound darkness.

The triplets' mouths slowly opened, in unison, their jaws cracking, their breath rank. An explosion of cockroaches poured out from their throats. The insects covered Nina's body, and fell onto the floor, thousands upon thousands. Piling up beneath her feet, a wave of them rose like a single massive creature, swirling around Nina, covering her legs, her chest, her face, seeking out the passageways of her mouth, her nostrils, her ears. She could feel them forcing their way inside her body, crawling underneath her skin, it felt like she was about to burst.

Her film-like vision worsened, a strobe effect taking over the room. She could hear, just faintly under the screaming, a projector whirring. Then her vision blurred even more, a melted film strip, dissolving into a blob of deep red...

***

...And then Nina was back at the store. Maggie stood in front of her, holding the headphone cord.

"Are you okay?" Maggie asked.

"What happened?"

"Jesus, Nina, you were screaming hysterically, then your eyes rolled back in your head. I thought you were having a seizure. You feel okay?"

Nina nodded. "I... I think so."

Maggie picked up a bucket of water and threw it onto Nina's face, soaking the upper half of her upper body.

"What the fuck, Maggie?"

Maggie jumped back, watching Nina.

"What the hell was that?" Nina asked.

"Holy water."

"What? When did you grab that?"

"Had to make sure."

"You only needed a few drops!"

Maggie smiled. "That was more fun."

Maggie undid the belts, freeing Nina. "So, what happened? How was it?"

Nina tried to answer but had to dive for a trashcan instead. She threw up for five minutes straight.

4.

The inside of the chapel had been transformed. Several followers filled trash bags with old blankets, dead rats, and empty beer bottles. Others scrubbed the place free of graffiti. The oak pews had been shoved against the outer walls. The hardwood floors had been swept and scrubbed, the scent of Pine-Sol hanging thick in the air. A large, muscular man stood on a tall ladder, inverting the massive cross hanging on the wall. He broke off the mahogany Jesus from its center and smashed it on the floor, its head and limbs scattering in different directions.

ManDown stood at the altar, reassembling his set-up from his bunker. Laptops, synths, turntables, and cords littered the platform. He was attempting to plug everything back in when he became dizzy. His stomach lurched; his knees locked. He gripped the edge of the altar with one hand to steady himself. The sanctuary spun around him. The old woman noticed, rushing over.

"Are you okay?" She led him to a short pew behind the altar.

ManDown sat, breathing deeply. He rubbed his temples. When he closed his eyes, he saw Nina, tormented by the triplets, the insects swarming her. As quickly as the vision had clouded his mind, it was gone. The blood rushed back to his head, and he could breathe again. What had it been? An omen? A warning?

"Master? Are you okay?" the woman whined.

"It's nothing. Back to work!"

The woman scurried away, her head down. ManDown went back to his laptop. He felt unsettled. Something didn't sit right within him. The vision hovered in the back of his mind, eating at him. He couldn't take any chances. They would have to work even faster. There was no more time to waste. It was now or never.

5.

Nina sat at Reggie's kitchen table, guzzling a large glass of water. Maggie wet a hand towel in the sink and dabbed Nina's forehead with it, then placed it around her neck, letting the cool water run down the back of her shirt. Maggie sat across from her.

"How're you feeling?" Maggie asked.

"Better. My head still feels like I drank a bottle of vodka last night, but it's better."

"So, you still think this will work?"

Nina tried to articulate her thoughts. "I think they weakened the demons when they made copies of the original three. Then, over time, the more of those copies Killian destroyed, the stronger the remaining ones became. And in turn, the demons, or the parts of them bound to the records, became more powerful, or at least more whole again, maybe? If he was right about the tethering, the semi-possession from listening, maybe I can do the opposite, dilute them, weaken them before ManDown can complete the ritual."

"By causing an epidemic of possessions?"

"Hopefully, if enough people hear it, it'll be more like a vaccine."

Maggie thought about that. "*If* you're right..."

"If I'm right..."

"It's a big if, Nina."

Nina reached across the table, took Maggie's hand in her own. Maggie was surprised but didn't let go. "This is dangerous, Maggie. I understand if you want to walk away."

Maggie placed her other hand on top of Nina's. "I think I'm in this for the long haul, as crazy as it sounds."

Nina smiled and squeezed Maggie's hand in thanks.

"You know what else this means?" Maggie asked.

"What?"

"It's a big day for someone," Maggie said teasingly. She grabbed her backpack and took out a laptop, setting it on the table. "Nina's very first computer."

"Oh no."

"But wait, there's more." Maggie pulled a smart phone from the top of her bag. She slid it across the table to Nina.

Nina ran her hands over it. "Fuck me."

Side D: Track 2: Prelude to the Fire (2:56)

1.

It was nearly time. Adrenaline coursed through ManDown as he worked the records. All three spun before him on the altar. Shadowy snakes rose from the circling grooves, moving up his arms. His hands no longer seemed to be under his control. Sinister beats blasted through massive speakers lining the walls of the sanctuary, the triplets chanting over deep, throbbing bass and synths.

A dozen followers ambled in a single-file line across the wooden floor. Their wrists slashed open, jagged wounds running up each of their arms. They held their hands out as they walked. Their blood stained the floor, painting an enormous crimson pentagram beneath their feet.

As ManDown raised the volume of the music, there was a faint flickering at the base of the upside-down cross. Just the hint of an immense doorway appeared, steeped in shadows. ManDown slowly brought down the volume, and the doorway disappeared, its glimmer fading with the music. ManDown smiled, fire blazing in his eyes. The ropes swirled around him, through him, clenching, unclenching, yearning for what was to come.

2.

Maggie stood before a large city map she'd taped to a wall in the record store. Nina had hauled all her equipment over from her apartment and was setting up her turntables and mixer on the store counter, connecting them to Maggie's laptop. The original records sat in a crate at her feet. Maggie placed another pushpin into a cluster on the map.

"There are six churches within ten miles, and four of them are closed," Maggie said over her shoulder.

Nina looked up. "Within ten miles of what?"

"ManDown's earliest known beats were for the Gacha Crew, right? They dropped their first mixtape when they were sixteen, and they went to high school here." Maggie pointed at the map, to the center of the circle of pins. "That's what started the whole idea that he was from here. People think he must have gone to school with them."

"And if he went to high school there, he probably grew up there."

"Exactly, nobody was bussing into that neighborhood for school."

"That's a great idea, Maggie. Nice work."

"*If* he didn't move."

"He's a recluse, like me. Hopefully, he didn't stray too far from home."

***

Maggie peered in the window of an old, boarded up church. She blew on the glass, rubbing it to see better inside. The church was dark, empty. The floor had rotted away at some point, falling into the basement beneath it. She walked the perimeter again, just to be sure. The exterior doors were locked and chained. It didn't look like anyone had been in there in years. She typed the next address into her phone and headed there on foot.

***

Nina was locked into her music. The program Maggie had downloaded was surprisingly user-friendly. Though slow-going, she was picking it up much quicker than she had anticipated. She wasn't ready to jump ahead thirty years in her beat-making tech just yet, but it was more tempting than she was ready to admit.

A slow, heavy beat played over the record store's speakers, a deep pipe organ sample, a loop of a choir singing in Latin. She slowly slid the bar on her mixer, and the crackle of record #2 emerged, the static transforming into the triplets screaming in a dead language.

Nina stopped the recording and took a step back from the counter. She took a few deep breaths, attempting to ease her headache by rubbing her temples. She closed her eyes, but when she did, the triplets were waiting for her, floating towards her with their black eyes. When she opened her eyes, a shadow moved in her periphery, a flash of a child's long hair, just out of sight down an aisle. Nina did a lap of the store to confirm she was indeed alone. Satisfied it was only in her head, she took a swig of the coffee she'd been chugging all day and got back to work.

***

Maggie passed a street corner, then doubled back. Her phone's map was a few seconds behind her actual movements. A few yards ahead of her, one of ManDown's followers, the elderly woman, stapled a red flyer to a telephone pole, a thick stack of them in her hand. She wore a long dress that had been blue at one point, but was now a muddy brown and torn to shreds. The elderly woman continued down the sidewalk, heading towards Maggie. She barreled straight ahead, as if in a trance. Maggie had to step to the side, out into the street, to avoid a collision with her.

"Hey! Watch it!" Maggie yelled.

The woman ignored her, or never heard her, and continued towards the intersection. Maggie hopped back onto the sidewalk. As she passed the telephone pole, she read the flyer:

MANDOWN – SYMPHONY OF SCREAMS VOL. III – HELL ON EARTH

FRIDAY – MIDNIGHT

WORLD PREMIERE – VIP LISTENING PARTY – LOCATION -??????

#HELLONEARTH

Maggie snatched the flyer from the pole, her heart racing. She spun around; the woman was nowhere in sight. Maggie sprinted back to the corner. The woman was already a block down, still stapling flyers.

Maggie followed her, trying to keep her distance, stopping at a bus stop, pretending to look at her phone. The woman quickened her pace, turned a corner, and disappeared.

Maggie jogged ahead to catch up and found herself in an empty alley. There was no sign of the woman, only the back doors of derelict businesses, a few dumpsters. Maggie crept forward slowly, checking the doorways carefully.

As Maggie passed a dumpster, the woman leapt out from behind it swinging a hammer. She just missed Maggie's head, the hammer head finding her collarbone instead, nearly fracturing it. They both fell to the pavement, the woman on top of her. Maggie twisted onto her back beneath her.

"Hey! I mean no harm!" Maggie screamed.

The woman straddled Maggie, her knees tight on her sides, crushing Maggie's ribs. She raised the hammer again, and Maggie gripped the woman's hand, bending her index finger back until it snapped. The woman howled, dropping the hammer. Maggie fumbled for it, but instead pushed it further away, just out of reach.

The woman covered Maggie's mouth with her other hand, leaning in close. Maggie struggled to free herself, to yell for help. The old woman was stronger than she looked. She could taste the sweaty filth from the woman's fingers on her lips. The woman locked eyes with her, eyes that were unblinking, bloodshot, crazed.

The woman opened her mouth as if to speak. Instead, massive cockroaches spilled out, piling onto Maggie's face and chest. Maggie could feel their tiny legs digging into her flesh, the warmth of their bellies chafing her skin. Maggie screamed, biting deep into the woman's fingers, her blood filling her mouth.

The woman squealed, yanking her hand back. Maggie backed up on her elbows and jumped to her feet, furiously brushing the cockroaches off her body. They skittered across the blacktop, seeking dark spaces to hide. Maggie spit on the ground repeatedly. The woman rose to her feet. Blood dripped from her hand, pooling on the ground. One cockroach stayed behind, braving the sunlight to lap it up.

They faced each other, a silent stand-off. The woman reached into a deep pocket on her dress and pulled out a machete. She took a step forward.

"Fuck this," Maggie muttered to herself as she turned and hauled ass out of there, flying down the alley towards the street, never looking back.

***

Nina and Maggie sat at Reggie's kitchen table. Maggie sipped on hot tea while Nina wiped her face with a wet towel.

"I want to dunk my head in a bucket of bleach," Maggie moaned.

"I'm so sorry."

"Will you be ready by tomorrow?"

Nina looked at the flyer on the table. "I'll have to be. I just hope it's good enough."

"It will be. You know it will be."

"A listening party. It's genius really, and keeping with his lo-fi style, the old-school flyers. I checked: #HELLONEARTH is already trending. There's an Instagram page with a countdown on it."

"I assume that's for the location?" Maggie said.

"You should lie down. At least one of us should get some sleep tonight, and I should get back to work."

3.

As dusk curdled the sky, a spiral of crows circled the chapel. The broken and cracked stained glass windows were teeming with insects: ants, beetles, roaches, flies, and maggots, all fighting for a good seat at the table. A stray dog ran by, terrified. He would only chance a quick glance at the building as he scampered on, the hair on his back raised, his tail down.

Inside, the party preparations were nearly complete. Massive red velvet curtains hung from the ceiling, covering the walls. Hundreds of unlit candles lined the perimeter, the altar, every available surface in the room. An old confessional booth, all dark wood and brass, had been transformed into a bar, fully stocked with top-shelf liquor, and huge glass bowls full of high-end drugs.

At each point of the enormous pentagram, a follower sat cross-legged, their eyes closed, their wrists slashed, pooling blood on the floor. Their bodies swayed to the deep, menacing beats crackling through the large speakers mounted on either side of the inverted cross, which had been inlaid with blazing red neon lights. Over the bass, the triplets spoke in tongues, sharing a laugh amongst themselves.

ManDown knelt before the cross, his eyes closed, his hands folded in prayer to his master. The ropes slithered and writhed on the floor. They circled around him, latching onto his limbs, lifting him high into the air. ManDown, floating, opened his eyes, and the all-consuming fire was so intense that the skin around his sockets blistered, his flesh melting down his face. He screamed at the cross, a thunderous clash of terror and ecstasy.

Side D: Track 3: Dueling Symphonies (7:27)

1.

Nina and Maggie stood at the store counter, too nervous to sit, their eyes glued to their phones. Maggie had spent the day scouring social media, refreshing her feed constantly while Nina had finished up her work. Maggie wanted to ensure they would be among the first to know the location of the listening party.

Nina was running on a toxic stew of caffeine, adrenaline, and little else. She had barely slept, and when she had nodded off, it was fleeting, the nightmares too much to bear. Nina hadn't told Maggie how much the records had affected her. She was scared Maggie would try and stop her from going through with it. They were so close to the end; she couldn't risk it. Nina stifled a yawn as she watched the sunset through a window. At least it would be over with soon, one way or another.

Maggie straightened up. "I got it! He posted it!"

"Where is it?"

"Intersection of 17th and Bryant."

"That's only a few miles away. Is there a church there?" Nina asked.

"No. I don't think so," Maggie checked the map on the wall. "Nothing that I can see."

"Maybe it's just the first step." Nina handed Maggie a USB stick. "I'll text you when it's time." Nina headed for the door.

"Be careful." Maggie called after her.

"You too."

2.

Nina hopped out of an Uber at the posted intersection. "I'll only be a few minutes. Big tip, five stars, okay?" The driver, a college student with bloodshot eyes, gave her a thumbs up and cranked up the radio.

A line of fans already snaked down the street, filling the sidewalk. Nina jogged over, securing her spot. There was a buzz in the air, the excitement and anticipation rippling through the growing crowd. Various conspiracy theories were being discussed ahead of her.

"Is this for real?"

"Could it be a hoax?"

"Will ManDown actually show?"

"Will he finally reveal his identity?"

Nina's stomach twisted as she listened. She wished she could tell them all to go home, that their lives were in danger, that they should get as far away from the city as they possibly could. She knew it wouldn't work. They'd think she was a plant, hired by ManDown himself. Or someone would film her pleas, post it online, and it would only make more people want to go. Besides, she felt like she needed to let it play out exactly as he planned it, if she wanted any chance of surprising him, of pulling this off.

Nina shuffled along the sidewalk, her impatience growing. Once there were only half a dozen fans in front of her, she could see the start of the line. A homeless man sat on an upside-down bucket, handing out glossy red envelopes. A high school kid took his envelope and opened it without moving, holding up the line.

"St. Michael's? Where's that? What's the fucking address, man?" the kid asked. The homeless man didn't respond. "C'mon dude, just tell me. How much you getting paid for this shit, anyways? You're just some fucking actor, right?"

The homeless man stood up, snatched the invitation out of his hands, and punched the kid in the face, hard. The kid staggered into the street, clutching his jaw, stifling tears. "What the fuck, dude? Who the hell do you think you are?" The kid scanned the crowd, silently pleading for help. No one took the bait, all eyes moving to the ground. The man lunged at him again, raising a fist, and the kid stumbled away, whimpering, his tail between his legs.

Nina reached the front of the line and grabbed her invitation, ripping it open as she made her way back to the Uber. Inside was a single sheet of thick black paper, emblazoned with flaked gold lettering:

ManDown cordially invites you to the Symphony of Screams, Vol. III
World Premiere Listening Party
Welcome to Hell on Earth
St. Michael's – Midnight

Nina hopped in her Uber, "Just a second." She typed St. Michael's church into her Maps. There was nothing close. Then she saw it, in the suggestions, St. Michael's Catholic school, listed as a closed business. It was just outside of Maggie's projected circle, a few miles from his suspected high school. Nina read the address to her driver, and texted Maggie an update.

3.

Rap-City Radio was buzzing as Maggie made her way through the hallways. The potential appearance by ManDown in their own city had been trending all day on social media. The higher-ups hoped it would translate into a bump in listeners that weekend. Maggie entered the office outside of the DJ booth, nodding at Matt, the intern, who was stuck working the night shift all weekend.

DJ Stacks was in the booth, speaking into the microphone with his deep, smooth, born-for-radio voice: "Pretty exciting night for hip-hop fans in Detroit, let me tell you. If you're not stuck in a glass box like me that is. Are the rumors true? Is ManDown actually playing live? Is Volume Three actually dropping at midnight? I'll believe it when I see it, folks, but rest assured, 89.3, your home for *real* hip-hop in the Motor City, will have boots on the ground there, reporting back live as it happens, or at least as close to live as we can get around here. While the true hip-hop heads wait with bated breath, here's a classic from the man himself to calm your nerves."

Stacks pressed play and leaned back, removing his headphones, taking a sip of water. Maggie was at the glass, tapping softly. She held up the USB stick, "Can I come in?" Stacks waved her through.

4.

Nina hopped out of the Uber at St. Michael's and jumped in another line, just beating a large group of drunk college students. She didn't expect anyone inside to be too concerned about capacity issues, but she couldn't risk getting turned away at the door. At least fifty people were ahead of her already, slowly shuffling forward, ducking through a hole in the fence guarded by two of ManDown's followers, both very large men. One of them took the invitations, tossing them into a bucket.

Nina leaned to one side, taking in the chapel on the other side of the fence. She could hear faint bass rumbling from inside, but not much else. With the velvet curtains blocking the windows, that was the only evidence of a clandestine gathering taking place. She scanned the block. ManDown had picked the perfect spot. The neighborhood seemed to be mostly empty, the houses boarded up. She wondered if any police would even bother to come and shut it down if someone called it in.

The sky was darkening, the clouds growing, churning, flashes of lightning bouncing between them. A large cyclone of crows circled above the chapel, more and more flocks arriving and joining them as Nina watched. Two guys ahead of her were passing a giant spliff back and forth, staring at the birds in awe. "A fucking legend, man," one said to the other, shaking his head, "How do you think he pulled that shit off?"

"He's a goddamn genius, that's how. Maybe CGI?"

Nina shook her head. These fools didn't stand a chance. If she was right about what was about to go down, she was going to be on her own in there. She felt something on her foot. She glanced down just in time to see a large cockroach scramble across the sidewalk, slipping underneath the fence. On the other side, it joined long lines of ants and roaches, all marching towards the chapel.

Nina got past the goons at the fence without incident and made her way inside. As she entered the sanctuary, the bass was overwhelming, booming more loudly than anything she had experienced in her life. She could feel it rippling her shirt, rattling her ribs. Red stage lights had been erected in each corner. They emitted an intense strobe light effect that bounced off the burning candles and velvet curtains, creating a disorienting light show against the glowing cross. Nina had to lower her eyes to avoid dizziness as she pushed her way through the crowd.

People were everywhere, crammed into the place, dancing, drinking. Dozens were crowded in front of the altar, snapping selfies, livestreaming everything. As Nina got closer to the altar, she saw that it was empty. The music was coming from an unattended laptop. She searched the crowd, but ManDown was nowhere to be seen. Stationed along the walls, guarding each exit, were more followers, homeless men and women positioned every few feet. Nina checked her phone, it was 11:51. She texted Maggie, *'I'm in. No sign of him yet. Be ready.'*

5.

Maggie read Nina's text, shoved her phone back in her pocket. She sat with Matt at his computer outside of the DJ booth. He eyed her with suspicion.

"You have to trust me on this, okay? Just do what I say, for the next few minutes." Maggie spoke firmly, daring him to question her.

"C'mon, how'd you pull this off? You really know him?"

"It's a long story. Can you hurry?"

Matt started to say something else but thought better of it. He inserted the USB into his tower.

6.

Nina forced her way through the crowd, looking for any sign of ManDown. People were packed tight into the sanctuary, with more pouring in. It was becoming harder and harder for Nina to power her way through the throngs of sweaty partiers. She was threading her way back towards the altar when the music cut out and the strobes stopped flashing, leaving the room bathed in a continuous, deep, crimson red.

The crowd exploded, chanting, "ManDown! ManDown! ManDown!" A door beneath the inverted cross opened, and ManDown emerged, his black hoodie up, a white ski-mask tight on his face, the eye openings soaked with blood. The throng grew louder, rushing forward, pressing against the short wall that held the altar. Nina planted her hands on the shoulders of two men squeezed in on either side of her, giving herself a boost as she jumped up and down, trying to see over the crowd. His followers shut all the exit doors, pushing back pissed off fans who were on the verge of getting in.

They locked the doors with chains and padlocks.

Nina texted Maggie, *'He's here. Do it.'* She put away her phone and removed the crucifix blade from her belt. She threw up her elbows, and forced her way towards the front, leaving a wake of dirty looks behind her.

7.

Maggie hovered behind DJ Stacks at the mic, a song fading out. He turned to her, "You're for real right? This is for real? This isn't a bit?"

Maggie nodded. "I'm not fucking you over, dude. It's legit."

The song ended and Stacks spoke into the mic, "Well, kids. Exciting news. We have a huge surprise for you here. Maggie, your usual drive-time-hostess-with-the-mostess, is with me now, and I'll let her do the honors." Stacks wheeled his chair back, and Maggie leaned forward, speaking into the mic.

"That's right, peeps, this is for everyone stuck at home, or stuck at work, wishing you were at the hip-hop event of the year. We have the world exclusive first track off ManDown's new record, Symphony of Screams, Volume Three! And to all the skeptics out there, this was given to me by the man himself. And I can confirm what we've all known from the start. He is one of Detroit's own! And for one night only, courtesy of the man himself, it's available for free download and streaming exclusively off our website! So spread the word, blow up that social! Grab it before it disappears. Without further ado, here it is!"

Maggie nodded at Matt through the glass. He pressed play, and Nina's track rattled through the speakers, its dark, ominous beats filling the room. It was an incredible beat, just like Maggie knew it would be, all pounding organs and dusty drums, sounding both old-school and futuristic at the same time. Underneath the rhythms, the triplets' voices emerged, samples of the three records playing, weaving in and out of the beat, their vocals chopped up, distorted. Maggie wanted to listen to more. It was the first of Nina's music that she had ever heard, but the triplets' voices were her cue. As Stacks nodded his head to the beat, Maggie shoved in a set of ear plugs and backed away towards the door.

"Sorry, Stacks. I can explain everything later. You just gotta trust me for now."

Stacks spun around in his chair. "What are you talking about?"

Maggie exited the booth and locked the door with a key. She grabbed a nearby chair and shoved it under the doorknob for good measure. Stacks stood up, his hands in the air. "Very funny, Maggie. It's almost my break. I need to piss!"

Maggie shook her head.

Matt stared at Maggie in disbelief. "Man, you better not lose me this internship."

8.

ManDown stood still behind his turntables, relishing in the adoration of the crowd. After a full minute of his fan's screams, he stepped forward, powering up his mixer. All three records began to spin, and the strobe lights flashed again. Sinister beats blasted out of the speakers, so loud Nina's ears rang. Deep bass pummeled the room again, shaking the floorboards beneath her. The crowd was in a frenzy, waves of people writhing to the beat.

Nina kept fighting her way to the front. The crowd was packed in even tighter around the altar, and she kept being shoved back. The temperature in the sanctuary was rising, sweat dripping down her back. Nina wasn't normally a claustrophobic person, but she felt it then, a panic welling up inside her.

ManDown's beats slowly faded away as he moved the crossfader, the static crackle of the records rising in volume to replace them. The triplets spoke, their voices echoing between the speakers surrounding the crowd. ManDown manipulated the records, scratching them, while weaving in MP3 recordings of them. He altered the pitch of the triplets' voices, playing some backwards, piling the voices on top of each other, overlapping tongues becoming a symphony of screams.

This had an immediate effect on Nina. Shadows invaded her vision, lunging at her, then fleeing backwards. A silhouette flew past her, climbing up the wall, onto the ceiling. It was one of the triplets, her eyes black, her mouth opened impossibly wide. Nina turned away and another triplet was right behind her, hiding behind a young woman, peering over her shoulder, sniffing the woman's hair. Nina shook her head. She couldn't allow them to distract her. She needed to stay focused. Nina fought her way through the crowd again, knocking people down to get through.

As the beats faded and the screams rose, the crowd slowed down, confused. Dancing gave way to nervous glances, a change in mood rippling through the crowd. A few people held their heads, pain swelling in their brains. A woman next to Nina doubled over, throwing up on the floor. Nina took advantage of the stilling bodies to get within a few feet of the altar.

ManDown took his hands off the turntables. They continued to spin, faster and faster, the voices growing louder and louder. He surveyed the crowd before him, ripped off his hoodie and yanked off his mask. His eyes were engulfed in flames, shooting from his sockets, his face a patchwork of horrific burns. Bloody ropes exploded from numerous open wounds in his chest, seeking the floor for leverage and lifting him up into the air. The crowd erupted into screams and panic, everyone scrambling back, a stampede seeking an exit that didn't exist.

Nina pressed herself tight against the altar to avoid the worst of it. She watched as the candles along the wall began to flicker. Behind ManDown, a massive doorway appeared. Wavering at first, then solidifying. The doorway was fifteen feet tall, filling the front of the sanctuary, blocking out the inverted cross. Nina could see shadows moving beyond it, crawling towards the threshold out of an infinite darkness.

9.

Maggie sat with Matt at his desk. Matt wore ear plugs as well. On the monitor, they watched a streaming/download counter on the radio station website. It was rocketing up by the hundreds. Maggie scanned her phone, scrolling social media sites.

"It's trending. Everybody's listening to it and loving it!" Maggie smiled; she was proud of Nina. She knew she could pull it off.

"This is the most traffic we've ever had. I hope we don't crash."

Maggie jerked her head up. "Wait… Is that possible?"

Matt shook his head. "I honestly don't know. Like I said, we've probably never had more than a hundred visitors in an entire day. So far, so good though."

They watched the numbers continue to rise. Maggie held her breath. In the booth behind them, DJ Stacks stumbled out of his chair onto his hands and knees. He grabbed a trash can and vomited. He stood up, wobbly, limping to the glass.

"What the hell is going on, Maggie? I don't feel so good." Stacks banged on the glass, trying the doorknob. "Let me outta here!"

Matt looked at Maggie. "Should we…"

"Just ignore him. It'll be over soon,"

Stacks yelled again, "At least turn this shit off! It's… I don't know. It just fucking hurts!"

Matt reached over to turn off the feed to the booth. Maggie grabbed his arm, stopping him. "You have to let it go. Keep it playing. It's our only chance. He needs to keep hearing it. Everyone does."

10.

Outside the chapel, the storm grew violent, loud cracks of thunder and blinding lightning pummeling the earth below. The clouds could finally take no more, sheets of rain poured down. The fans left locked outside scattered into the night, seeking shelter. The rain slowly turned a deep, thick red, soaking the chapel roof in blood. The followers stationed outside gathered together and held hands. They lifted their faces up to the sky and opened their mouths, drinking it in.

Cockroaches spilled from their throats, seeking to quench their own insatiable thirst.

Inside, terror mounted. The crowd clamored for the exits, but the followers stood guard, shoving them back, beating anyone to the floor who tried to pass. The elderly woman guarded her door with her machete and her hammer, slashing and pummeling anyone who got too close.

The black doorway grew wider, fully solidifying. Once it did, the shadows from the other side broke through. Hundreds of tendrils made of black smoke spilled over the threshold. The snakes slithered through the sanctuary, forcing themselves down the throats of anyone they could corner. Once the snake was inside, the host would drop, shaking on the floor as though in seizure. After a few seconds they sprang back to their feet, reborn, their eyes black, flames flickering behind them.

The portion of the crowd that was still human continued to stampede the exits, banging helplessly on the stone walls, screaming for help. Candles were trampled and kicked over, setting the velvet curtains on fire. Flames quickly shot up the thick fabric, licking the large wooden beams crisscrossing the ceiling. The cramped sanctuary grew even hotter, the oxygen eaten by the fire.

A possessed man lunged at Nina. One hand gripped her neck, the other clawed at her face, her eyes. He grabbed her lower jaw, yanking her mouth open. Nina looked up. A smoke snake high above them began to descend, spiraling towards her open mouth. Nina gripped her crucifix blade tightly and shoved it into the man's stomach, burying it behind his ribcage. He squealed in pain and let go, collapsing onto the floor. He writhed on his back, his exposed skin blistering, cracking open. The smoke snake fled his mouth, shooting towards her. Nina ducked as it passed her by, on fire, seeking a new host.

Nina jumped onto the altar, only a few feet from ManDown. He floated back down, a smile on his melted face. "Glad you could join us, Nina." Nina tightened her grip on her blade and took a step towards him.

11.

Stacks tapped his forehead against the glass, gently at first, his eyes wide, crazed, his mouth crumpled, as if he was on the verge of tears. "Turn it off!" He slammed his head, harder and harder, opening a small cut. A trickle of blood dripped down the glass.

"Shouldn't we help him?" Matt asked.

"We can't. Not yet. He should get better once it's done," Maggie replied.

"You sure?"

"No."

"So, what if he doesn't?"

"We call a priest?"

"A priest? What the fuck's going on, Maggie? I can't lose this gig. My parents will kill me. I need these credits to graduate."

"I'll write you a glowing recommendation. Just make sure this shit doesn't crash."

Outside, Maggie could hear sirens on the street. She went to the window. Two cop cars had pulled up, surrounding a teenager sitting on the curb. Maggie opened the window to hear. The cops slowly approached the kid, guns drawn. He swayed back and forth, large headphones cupping his ears.

"Everything okay, son? We've had a few complaints about you," a cop asked.

The teenager looked up, his body swaying. "Don't you hear them?"

"Hear who?"

"The children. The precious little girls?"

The officers exchanged dubious looks.

"Uh, no, can't say that I do. Let us get you some help here, son."

The kid jumped to his feet, staring at something behind the officers. He ripped off his headphones and pointed at the empty street. "They're here! They're coming for you! They're coming for us all!" The cops looked behind them, and the kid took off running, screaming as he sprinted down the sidewalk. The cops holstered their weapons and took off after him on foot.

"What's going on down there?" Matt asked.

"Nothing. Just some kid."

Maggie's stomach was in knots. If Nina was wrong, what had they just unleashed upon the world?

12.

ManDown raised a wrist to his mouth, biting deeply into his flesh. Threads of skin stuck in his teeth as he pulled his arm away from his charred face. He held the open wound over the turntables, blood pouring onto the records. They began to spin even faster, sucking his blood into the grooves.

The doorway grew even larger, filling the entire wall of the sanctuary. The fog billowing through it had dissipated. Beyond it, a dark figure, a great looming shadow, approached the threshold. ManDown scowled at Nina, his mouth dripping red.

"You're too late. You can't stop us know. He'll be here soon." ManDown growled, his voice now the voice of three, in unison.

ManDown suddenly recoiled, his body shaking, as if he had just absorbed a blow from an invisible foe. He stumbled back, plopping down onto a pew.

Nina moved closer. "You sure about that?"

ManDown shook again, a violent spasm.

The hulking shadow grew even larger, lumbering closer to the doorway. Nina knew she was running out of time. The ropes swirled around ManDown, trying to prop him up, but they were weakened too, they couldn't support his weight. ManDown clutched his chest, then his temples.

"What have you done?" he asked.

Nina held up her cell phone. "You're going viral." Nina checked the website. "Wow, ten thousand downloads already. Your fans have been waiting a *really* long time for this."

13.

Maggie and Matt watched the download numbers continue to sky-rocket as word spread around the world, the tally passing twenty thousand and counting. Maggie went to the glass; DJ Stacks lay on an old couch in the corner. He was still out of it, but he seemed calmer, his eyes less bloodshot.

Maggie rushed to the window. The cops were dragging the teenager towards their car in cuffs. He, too, seemed less agitated. He looked around, blinking, wondering aloud. "Where am I? What happened?"

A cop scoffed at the question and shoved him in the back of a squad car. "Nice try, kid."

Maggie was ecstatic, "I think it's working!"

14.

Nina shoved her phone in ManDown's face. "Thirty thousand!"

ManDown forced himself to stand. He lunged at her, clumsily, his legs giving out. Nina stepped back and let him collapse at the base of the altar. He twisted onto his back, writhing in agony, the demons inside him pulled in thirty thousand different directions and counting. His body buckled, his limbs stretching, his bones cracking, his skin splitting apart. Chunks of flesh broke off his body, scattering across the altar floor. An army of roaches swarmed the altar, picking up the tiny morsels of skin and muscle, fighting over them as they scurried away to a dark corner to feast.

The ropes twisting around his body suddenly went slack. Nina leapt on top of him and buried the dagger between the loose ropes, deep inside his chest. ManDown's body burst into flames beneath her. Nina scrambled away; her eyebrows singed. ManDown's flaming body exploded, a billowing fireball, showering Nina in blood and guts.

The doorway was still open, the shadow crossing the threshold. A gigantic, wet, coal-black hand reached through, its swollen digits thick beneath layers of scorched skin. A loud, bellowing roar filled the room. The possessed immediately swiveled towards the doorway, dropping to their knees, bowing their heads in reverence.

Nina jumped to her feet and kicked the turntables off the altar. Silence filled the space as she yanked out every cable she could find, smashing ManDown's laptop on the floor. She leaped down from the altar, stomping on the records, reducing them to shards. Shadow snakes shot out of them, striking at her, searing her legs.

Behind her, the doorway flickered. The possessed all turned their heads towards Nina. Furious, they rose to their feet, rushing her, surrounding her. She tried to fight them off with the dagger, but they wrested it from her hands. They clawed at her face, pulling her down to the floor, then raising her up over their heads, attempting to tear her limb from limb.

The doorway shrank rapidly, its edges shriveling towards the center like curtains closing. One by one, the shadowy snakes were jerked out of their hosts, wrenched from their throats, sucked back through the closing doorway. Their former hosts collapsed onto the ground, gasping for breath. Nina fell to the floor, nearly landing on her head. The shadow pulled back, but the doorway closed too quickly. Its blackened hand was severed at the wrist, falling to the floor with a thud. The bellowing roar was instantly snuffed out, replaced by the chaos in the room.

Nina forced herself up. The fire had spread from the curtains to the rafters, the smoke thick and heavy. She choked as she stumbled through the confused swarms of people, searching for the nearest exit. The followers who had been guarding them were now piles of insects, gigantic swarming mounds, eating themselves from the inside out. She yanked on the thick chains locked around the bar across the door, the padlock holding firm.

She grabbed a man standing near her, still in a daze, shaking his shoulders. "Help me! Grab this pew!" He finally heard her, snapping out of his stupor. They lifted a pew that had been shoved up against the wall. As they struggled with it, others near them joined in the effort. Together, they turned the pew into a battering ram. After numerous hits, the chain gave way, and the door separated from the frame, flying into the dirt outside.

The crowd spilled out of the exit, tripping over themselves to get away from the smoke that billowed out behind them, chasing them into the dark.

Above the chapel, the storm was clearing, and the crows were flying away. Nina stumbled through the crowd. Behind her, the chapel windows shattered, flames pouring out from inside, igniting the exterior of the building. She made it through the fence and collapsed on the curb. Sirens roared in the distance.

"Nina? Nina!"

Nina stood up, scanning the street. Maggie emerged from the crowd, running towards her. She embraced Nina, a long hug.

"Is he dead?" Maggie asked.

"Pulled apart in thirty thousand directions," Nina answered, her voice like sandpaper.

"Over fifty thousand now. You're really sweeping the nation."

Nina laughed, and then leaned into Maggie, kissing her.

Maggie returned it, deeply, then pulled back, looking her over. "Is that blood? That's fucking disgusting!" Maggie wiped her mouth on her sleeve.

Nina attempted another laugh, but it turned into a harsh cough, doubling her over. Maggie led her down the street, her arm tight around her shoulder. "Let's get you out of here."

Side D: Outro: A Grand Re-Opening (2:36)

1.

The cemetery was empty as Nina made her way through the endless rows of gravestones. The sun was still rising, just peeking over the horizon, the trees casting long shadows across the lawn. Nina found her parents' graves and sat cross-legged before them. She pulled dead flowers from a vase and replaced them with a fresh bouquet.

She sat there in silence, taking in the fresh air, moving her palms through the blades of grass. As the sun rose higher and hit her cheek, she closed her eyes and felt its warmth. Even during the day, the echoes of what she experienced still coursed through her. She tried to keep a brave face for Maggie, but Nina knew she wasn't healed yet.

Nina wasn't sure if she ever would be. She still felt the weight of the triplets, and what possessed them, heavy on her soul. She still saw shadows in her peripheral vision, a darkness that seemed to stay just beyond her reach, just out of her sight. Silence was still not her friend. If it got too quiet, she was sure she could hear the girls' whispers, beckoning to her. Lying in bed at night, with ear buds in, unable to sleep, she was still certain that she could hear the girls, just over the din of her music.

When she finally found sleep, it wasn't pleasant. Most nights, the triplets followed her there as well. Sometimes she would spend the night in their bedroom, in that decaying farmhouse in Maine, watching them wreak havoc on that poor old man. When they were done with him, they would move onto her, toying with her at first, before slowly tearing her body apart, limb by limb. Other nights she would be joined by ManDown himself, reliving the chaos of the sanctuary, the hordes of the possessed piling on top of her, clawing at her body, her face, until she woke up screaming, drenched in sweat. Sometimes, she would simply be alone, falling in the dark, an endless chasm below her, welcoming her.

When Nina's nightmares finally jolted her awake, Maggie would always be there, ready to embrace her. Nina didn't know what she would do without her. They were taking it slow, reconnecting and rebuilding what they had once shared together. Nina was confident they were on the right track, and she was determined not to make the same mistakes again. She was never going to take Maggie for granted, and she would hold onto her tightly for the rest of her life.

Physically, Nina was doing better. Her fatigue was lessening, despite the sporadic slumber. The bruises covering her body were healing. At some point in the chapel, she had broken a rib. That was doing better too. So were her lungs. She was coughing up less and less blackened phlegm each morning, the effects of the smoke inhalation gradually fading.

Nina stared at the gravestones in front of her. The events of the past weeks had provided Nina with the perfect opportunity to avoid her grief, to sidestep the fact that both of her parents were now dead. The new stillness in her life allowed that unfortunate reality to return.

But with Maggie's help, Nina had found something to keep herself busy. Together, they had applied for a small-business loan, and miraculously, the bank had given it to them. It didn't hurt that the manager was a self-professed vinyl-junkie who had frequented her father's store over the years. He saw the same untapped potential that Nina always had and agreed to the loan on the spot. Nina and Maggie were now officially the owners of a completely revamped Round-A-Bout-Reggie's.

She checked her watch, it was time to get going, she didn't want to be late. Nina reached out, touching her father's headstone. Nina spoke softly, "It's the big day, dad. I hope I can do right by you. And also, full disclosure, we made a few changes, so no haunting my ass, okay? I already have too much of that shit in my life as it is."

2.

Nina jogged down the sidewalk, juggling two large coffees, trying not to spill them, failing miserably at it. As she rounded the corner, she stopped in her tracks, in shock. There was a long line of customers outside the store, already half-way down the block. Nina held back tears as she passed the growing crowd. The old-school customers recognized her, shouting her name as she flew by.

The outside of Round-A-Bout-Reggie's was largely the same, other than a new coat of paint on the sign, and a massive banner Nina had hung with Maggie's help, exclaiming *'GRAND RE-OPENING!! –*

SATURDAY!! – RECORD STORE DAY!! - FREE T-SHIRT WITH EVERY PURCHASE!!' Inside, more changes would be noticeable to its regulars. For one, it was cleaner than it had been in decades. Also, for the first time, there was a large section of new-release vinyl records, all genres of music fully stocked, with an emphasis on golden-age hip-hop.

In addition to that, Nina had devoted a large corner of the shop to local artists, selling an assortment of paintings, pottery, homemade incense, candles, and more. Nina's favorite addition by far though, was a large mural of her father, painted on the wall behind the counter. Nina had commissioned it from an artist friend she had known since high school. As a source, the artist used a photograph Nina had always cherished, captured at a family dinner: Reggie mid belly laugh, his infectious smile on full display.

Maggie was behind the counter, watching a Detroit nightly news clip on her phone, *'...Authorities still have no explanation for the wave of sickness and violence that spread last month following the release of what would turn out to be music producer ManDown's last song. Police have confirmed that his remains were recovered in the St. Michael's fire, where an apparent illegal listening party for his new album ended in flames and tragedy. Those who were affected have seemingly recovered, and no new cases have been reported, although many still face serious charges...'* Nina flew through the front door, locking it behind her. Maggie quickly tossed her phone on the counter.

"Did you look outside?" Nina asked, handing Maggie a coffee.

"They've been here for hours, Nina. Just like I told you they would be."

"I can't believe it."

"People loved your dad, and they want you to succeed too."

Nina put an arm around Maggie, squeezing her tight. "Thank you, I couldn't have done this without you."

"Damn right."

Nina burst out laughing. She let go of Maggie, and started to ready the counter, double-checking the till, the connection on their credit card reader.

"I heard back from Molly."

Nina froze, her heartrate rising. Molly was a friend of a friend. She ran a local music venue and bar. Maggie knew her better than Nina, mostly through the radio station. They had put on a few events together over the years.

"What'd she say?" Nina asked.

"She hated it."

"I knew it."

"Oh my God, Nina. I'm joking! You got it."

"For real?"

"Of course. She loved your mixtape, just like I told you she would. You've got Thursday nights, ten to midnight, on a trial basis."

"Holy shit."

"Yep, you just got yourself a real DJ gig."

"Well, now I'm fucking terrified."

"You're gonna kill it. Your track is still streaming everywhere. No one is even questioning if it's him or not, one of the greatest hip-hop producers of all time."

"Okay, okay, one thing at a time. I can have a panic attack about that news later. Right now, I need to focus on my current, opening day panic attack."

Nina and Maggie stared at the front of the store, a long line of eager customers in the windows, peering back, checking their watches, attempting to see inside.

"You ready?" Maggie asked.

Nina took a deep breath, facing the mural, her father smiling down on her.

"Let's do this."

45rpm 7-Inch - Bonus Track: Occulto Cinepresa (ManDown Remix) (2:58)

1.

Niccolo was having a bad semester at school. His grades had been slipping for weeks, and a worried professor had notified his parents, who were now justifiably concerned. This was not like Niccolo, who had been a straight-A student his whole life. Now he found himself a failing sophomore at the Pontifical Lateran University in Vatican City, just outside of Rome.

Niccolo sat on a campus bench, the sun beginning to set. He knew he should be catching up on his philosophy homework, but he also knew that wouldn't be happening anytime soon. He wore headphones, something he had done non-stop for weeks. Nina's track played loudly in his ears, over and over, on repeat. Niccolo's second passion, after philosophy, was hip-hop, and he had been one of the first in the world to download the fake ManDown track the night it went live.

Niccolo was one of the unfortunate listeners deeply affected by the recording. He experienced vivid, nightmarish hallucinations, and spent several minutes in his dormitory being perused by phantoms of the demonic triplets. When the effects finally waned, watered down by the spread of the track, Niccolo came to, and found himself on the roof of his dorm, one foot hanging over the edge, ready to plunge to his death ten stories below.

Since that night, Niccolo's obsession with ManDown had only increased. He found himself at the bottom of countless rabbit-holes online, absorbing everything known about the man, his music, and the bizarre circumstances surrounding his death. His browser history was a checklist of Reddit pages and music forums, with subheadings such as: *'ManDown's True Identity'*, *'ManDown Sample Sources'*, *'ManDown's True Cause of Death?'*, *'Biblical Sources in ManDown's Discography'*, *'Possession Plague Cover-Up?'*, *'Why is the Catholic Church Lying to Us?'*, *'Who was Abraham Martel?'*

As the track started over again in his ears, the triplets seemed to speak directly to him. Niccolo could never quite make it out, but he was convinced that they were trying to tell him something or show him something. He was sure that they needed his help, and he was right.

Niccolo opened his eyes to a dark, nearly empty campus. He looked around, in a daze; he had lost several hours again. His headphones had died a long time ago, but Nina's track still reverberated in his head, bouncing around his skull. The triplets told him to stand up, and he listened.

2.

Niccolo snuck around to the back of the University's library building, crouching in the shadows. A security guard strolled down the sidewalk, making his nightly rounds. Niccolo waited several minutes before approaching a utility entrance. He grabbed a fist-sized rock from the landscaped tree line along the building and broke a small pane of glass on the door.

Niccolo's eyes slowly adjusted to the darkness as he made his way through a gargantuan library several stories high. Once he was deep within the heart of the library, far from any windows, he flicked on his phone's flashlight. He was being drawn to something, he just didn't know what it was yet, an invisible tether pulling him towards an unknown fate.

Niccolo took a set of stairs down to a lower level. It was filled with the library's less popular items, old cassettes, CDs, VHS tapes, microfilm, everything that was requested less and less by students and scholars as newer technologies replaced them. Niccolo scoured a dark corner with his flashlight, scanning shelves of film containers. One box, covered in a thick layer of dust, called to him. A single yellowing index card was stapled to it. It read: *'Abraham Martel Trial Evidence, Box #4'*. He gently removed it from the shelf, setting it on the floor. He didn't need to open it; the triplets had already told him what he would find inside.

3.

Niccolo set up a 16-millimeter projector on the desk in his dorm room. He lived in a single apartment with no roommates, an upgrade from freshman year that took a lot of whining to his parents to obtain. He pulled his twin bed away from the wall and taped a white bedsheet to the painted cinderblocks. Double-checking a curled, yellowing manual he found at the bottom of the case, he gently threaded a reel of film through the projector.

Niccolo shut off his overhead light and flipped the switch on the projector. It came to life, its aging fan spewing out a cloud of dust as it spun the reel, pulling the brittle, cracking film past the lens. On the screen, a flickering blur began to play. Niccolo twisted the lens, bringing the film into focus.

At first, the film was only a static shot of a dark wood paneled wall. Then a hand reached into frame, opening a small rectangular door, revealing an open hole in a knot of wood. The film zoomed in, through the hole, into the room beyond, the triplets' bedroom.

It was the entire failed Martel exorcism, filmed in jerking black and white. Father Chabot towering over the triplets, reading the rites, shaking the holy water, the girls writhing beneath their ropes, then overpowering him, tearing his body apart.

After Chabot was dead and in pieces, the triplets' bodies went limp, their physical forms finally failing from the many days of unceasing, unadulterated terror. Their mouths went slack, opening wide, in unison. Three black shadow snakes rose from their throats, escaping their doomed vessels. They circled the room, moving frantically. The gramophone still spun record #3. The snakes were drawn to it and the other two records lying on the table, each one seeking its own refuge beneath the coal-black grooves.

The film ended, a blinding, flickering light, and Niccolo quickly shut it off. His head pounded; his heart raced in his chest. The whispers grew louder inside the room, instructing him.

4.

Niccolo spent the next week learning a music program on his laptop. Slowly, and with great difficulty, he was able to isolate the different audio tracks within Nina's beat. He separated the triplets' voices from the music, piecing them back together.

By the time he was finished, Niccolo was fully in a trance-like state, having not slept or eaten in several days. He started up the film on the projector and pressed play on his laptop. As the triplets screamed on screen, the audio began, syncing perfectly with the film.

Niccolo stood, drawn to the flickering light. Mesmerized by the fusion of image and sound, he reached out, his hand touching the sheet, caressing the faces of the girls. As he did, the film jerked, skipped, then melted, a crimson blob filling the screen. The audio slowed down with it, the triplets' voices deepening, distorting. Niccolo stepped back in alarm.

Black smoke snakes shot out of the melting screen, attacking Niccolo. He dropped to the floor as the tendrils burrowed into his mouth and nostrils, overtaking him. When Niccolo opened his eyes, they burned bright with blinding flames. He clutched his temples, screaming in agony. A rope burst forth from his belly, twisting around his chest, silencing his cries. Niccolo blinked rapidly. There were shadows in the room with him, three of them. They shot forward, screaming, consuming him, plunging him into darkness.

"Aperi Ianuam!"

About the Author

Bryan Holm was born and raised in Minnesota and lives in St. Louis Park with his wife and dog. He once toured the Coen brother's childhood home under the pretense of purchasing it, in hopes he could absorb whatever alchemy led to their genius. It didn't work. He is a photographer by day who spends his nights writing and consuming all things horror. His short fiction has been published in anthologies by Sinister Smile Press, Eerie River Publishing, Strange Wilds Press, Dead Sky Publishing, and HellBound Books. He was featured on the Bloodlist as a Fresh Blood Selects for his screenwriting. More info at www.bryanholm.com.

Instagram: @holmbry

Bluesky: @holmbry.bsky.social

www.ingramcontent.com/pod-product-compliance
Lightning Source LLC
Chambersburg PA
CBHW071421300726
48976CB00004B/1197